THE GENTLEMAN

The Adventures of a Tech Casanova

*Silicon Valley Tech Billionaire by Day. Erotic
Thrill-Seeker by Night.*

To Leena. To a Sagittarius, your soul, and your sexuality.

Contents

Foreword

We are incredibly excited to announce the release of our second book, now available to readers around the world. It has been two years since the release of our first publication, which chronicled the powerful and transformative journey of a Hong Kong woman who joined our community. Through her involvement with us, she discovered her inner voice, redefined her sense of self, and embarked on a personal mission that continues to inspire many. Her story was one of exploration, empowerment, and bold self-expression, and we are delighted to bring you something equally exciting and provocative with our latest release.

While we are perhaps best known for hosting our signature orgy parties in Hong Kong, Australia, and the United Kingdom, our mission goes far beyond these electrifying events. At the heart of everything we do is a core belief: we strive to "make the world better"—not through conflict, but through love. Our philosophy is simple but profound: promote intimacy, connection, and passion, while fostering a culture that celebrates openness and embraces the full spectrum of adult experience. We bring this philosophy to life through a variety of mediums—each designed to engage, educate, and entertain our diverse and ever-growing audience. Whether it's through erotically charged stories that spark the imagination, sensual movie reviews that explore the boundaries of desire, or musical collaborations with

both mainstream pop stars and indie artists that dive deep into adult themes, we are constantly pushing the envelope. Beyond entertainment, we also offer regular updates on the Japanese AV scene, provide comprehensive sex education, and host workshops that delve into the complexities of LGBTQ+ relationships and the dynamic world of BDSM.

In 2023, we had the unique pleasure of welcoming a remarkable figure into our community: "The Gentleman." As his name suggests, he embodies everything you would expect from a true modern British Casanova—refined, charismatic, and effort-lessly seductive. His presence in our club was unforgettable, and his influence undeniable. It wasn't long before he expressed his desire to document his experiences within our world, to capture the essence of what we do through his own lens. When he came to me with this idea, I immediately said, "Why not?"—and from that moment on, things moved quickly. His narrative was too tantalizing, too evocative to be confined to just the written word.

For those of you who are intrigued by what we do, or are simply curious to learn more about the enigmatic "Gentleman" who has captured so much attention, this book offers a tantalizing glimpse into our world. It is an invitation to explore our community and its secrets, where passion, desire, and self-expression are celebrated in their fullest forms. Whether you're a longtime follower of our work or discovering us for the first time, we hope this book inspires you to embrace your own journey of exploration and connection.

Founder of HKSP,

Mary

Introduction

You know *that* feeling when you're horny.

Where your lips become dry and salty. When your eyes gloss over and you become an animal. Where you forget all your inhibitions. And there's a hunger inside you.

We all experience that. It's all part of our biology. Our wiring.

That is being sexual. But we live increasingly in a sanitised sexual world.

I know there's porn. There's plenty of that, just a Google search away.

From PornHub to Miss AV to OnlyFans. Plenty of gigabytes and terabytes freely available on the internet for every man to have a wank and every woman to have some fun.

There's plenty of skin.

Young girls these days love to show skin and their shortest skirts. Men show off their abs and pecs freely without prompting.

There's plenty of fucking.

We all hear about which startup founder or celebrity is fucking who. People discuss how many times they're fucking a week and we all want to increase our body count.

But what I'm talking about is being *sexual.*

Like charming a woman, knowing that both partners know what they want, and the night's foray is to get closer to it.

Like the foreplay of kissing and connecting, and touching and teasing.

Like eating pussy, both the taste, the texture, the feeling.

Like caressing a woman and seeing her grasp the bed, to call your name. To focus on both your pleasure and hers, at the same time.

This is being sexual. And there is nothing wrong with wanting to feel sexual.

Sex is life. Being sexual is the essence of life. It's the core of what we are. As animals. As bodies. Our natural drive.

To deny that drive, to cower before it, to be afraid of it, is to deny our very own humanity. To want to submit to our very being.

We must not. We must own our sexuality.

To know what feels good and makes us horny.

To know what turns us on, and off.

To acknowledge it and be ok expressing it. And to embrace it.

Because then you're really embracing who you truly are. As an animal, as a person, and as living energy.

I lived and wrote the following stories to embrace what I truly am. These stories are all based on real interactions, real people, and real situations. They explore my past year's adventures - physically, mentally, energetically, and sexually.

I have anonymized myself, my lovers, and the other people involved. The Valley, at the end of the day, is small. People know each other. People talk. You run into the same circles time and time again.

I would rather not have to discuss my life and instead focus on my startup. So it is not without risk that I share these stories and adventures.

But the risk is worth the energy and the philosophy of being open and fully embracing what I am.

I hope you enjoy these stories as much as I had making them.

1

The Pinot Grigio

I receive a text message from Panda. On Telegram.

"Come over tonight. At Raffles Hotel."

It's the first time I've received anything from Panda since she interviewed me.

I still remember her interview for the swingers club a few months back, where we video conferenced over Telegram.

"So you like sex, do you?" she asked.

"Well yes, sure I do. Who doesn't?" I responded cheekily.

And we went on from there.

And tonight's finally the night.

It's a hot day in Singapore, one of those steamy, tropical days

where just going outside is like going into the sauna. I stay in our newly constructed office most of the day, only venturing out briefly to get some white wine for tonight.

A New Zealand pinot grigio. Super cold and crisp. To cut the humidity, density, and heat.

And to avoid being drenched in sweat and ruining my Holland & Sherry jacket, I take the typical blue Singaporean taxi to the hotel.

I arrive. I go past the colonial–style fans, the distinctive white walls, the Long Bar.

I check my Telegram.

905.

I press the wooden elevator button up and head upstairs.

* * *

I stand in front of room 905. There's a nervous energy inside me.

This is the first time I've had group sex. Would it be a few girls? A few guys? Can I get it up in front of the other guys?

Doubts flood my mind. My palms are a bit sweaty, my stomach in a bit of a knot.

5

Would I recognize anyone? Would they recognize me? Would my cock be enough?

A rush of blood to my head.

Though I have to admit - I like the feeling. I feel alive, I feel like I'm doing something I wanted to do for so long.

To submit to my very desire. To be ok with my sexuality. To feel alive, to feel doubts, and to overcome them.

To make this all normal.

I ring the doorbell.

* * *

Inside there's already a young lady and a man, both naked under the covers. And Panda, who is facilitating this session.

Panda facilitates by making sure all participants are having fun. If anything goes out of hand, she can interject.

This is done for the lady's protection, of course.

"Reasonable," I think to myself.

I crack open the screw-top Pinot Gris. I made sure to go for the new style, otherwise you never know if the hotel room has a corkscrew. And if they don't, you don't have to call room service.

I offer everyone a drink. Only Panda, responsible as she is, declines.

The young lady accepts my glass and introduces herself. "Miao Miao," she says.

"Pussy," I think.

I like Miao Miao. Cute face, thin body, tight. Something easy to throw around.

The other gentleman introduces himself as well. "James," he offers.

"We're supposed to start with a massage," Panda suggests, "but why don't you shower first."

I agree.

Perhaps it's my smell. I don't think I smell particularly bad. So it's likely hygiene.

I hang my Holland & Sherry and white dress shirt, and set aside my Rolex GMT on the marble wash basin. I wash my hair, shaved body, and shaved cock and balls. After the stifling Singaporean heat, it feels good to get a cold shower in.

I come out and dry myself with the plush Egyptian cotton towels. You can always tell a 5 star hotel from others by the little things, like the towels. And the bedsheets.

I come back to the bed, where Miao Miao and James are still just chatting. They haven't started yet. Just waiting for me.

I feel honoured.

"Why don't you start by massaging Miao Miao," Panda suggests, talking to me as if I'm a virgin.

I dutifully comply.

Miao pulls down the covers, highlighting her B-cup breasts and slim waistline. She doesn't have a completely shaved pussy, but it's manicured.

Her total package is easy on the eyes.

I massage Miao Miao, going through the motions on her arms, to her back, and down to her ass. I get to the point where the ass melts into the legs, where her pussy is.

And my eyes lock in.

There's something about a man and a pussy. A man can act all coy about seeing breasts and tits, but the sight of a pussy can drive a man insane.

Pussies can run in various shapes and sizes. Large, labia lips to thin, little ones. Ones that are flappy and ones that are tight.

Then there's the clit, the cute, little button that emerges from the hood if all is successful.

8

But that's all just foreplay.

There's a whole new world once you go inside the pussy itself, when it's just starting to get wet. And then you can insert your tongue and fingers inside, playing with the moisture, the fleshy, juicy part inside. Or taste the moist, sweet nectar.

But it's the moment that the pussy gets wet that is the crowning moment.

Because you're the one that made her horny. You're the one that made her body crave sex.

And today, I'm going to eat Miao Miao's pussy until her body craves sex. Not crave. Needs.

I start with her labia, which is nice and thin. I lick them gently, first the right side, and then the left.

I work my way down to the bottom of her pussy, where it meets the space between that and her asshole. I flick my tongue there, prolonging my flicking.

Miao Miao shudders slightly.

I move back up, my thick tongue tip separating her labia lips as I lick upwards to her clit, making sure I stop just shy of it.

I do this twice. Thrice. Four times.

Miao Miao shakes again.

I pause. I gauge her pussy's wetness before I lick upwards again. I think there's something.

I taste a sweet nectar on this time's lick. Mixing with my saliva, slightly sticky.

Mm. This tastes good.

"Uuggghhhh," Miao Miao lets out.

Ah yes, I'm turning her on.

I double my effort on her snatch, increasing the sounds of me sucking, wanting to create sounds of sex to stimulate her senses.

"Mmmm," Miao Miao moans, wriggling her legs and opening her pussy even wider for me to do my work.

I continue to eat, now moving up to her clit and sucking the little pearl out of its hood. Every so often, I go back to my long, deep, full-tongued fucks where I slightly penetrate her as I lap up.

Miao Miao's moans increase in both volume and frequency. And in carnal desire.

James, in the meantime, is getting sucked off by Miao Miao. Wonderfully, even.

But I don't care. I'm channelling my energy, my intention, my focus.

All on eating her pussy.

2

A Baijiu

Panda excitedly types on Telegram. "Did you enjoy your last time with Miao Miao?"

You can almost hear the klickety klack of her fingernails hitting the keys of her iPhone.

"I did," I reply, "She was a darling."

"Well, she's free next week if you are?" Panda klacks back.

"I'm in Beijing though," I retort. I'm there to headline a tech conference, but I don't mention that.

"No worries, she can meet you there," Panda quickly klacks, "if you want her to."

* * *

I'm put up at the Aman Summer Palace, a beautiful venue right

next to the Forbidden Palace. And I managed to get some *baijiu*, a local liquor in China.

China has three main types of liquors - *baijiu*, *huangjiu*, and *mijiu*. *Baijiu*, or white wine, is usually made from sorghum and known for the famous brand Moutai. *Huangjiu*, or yellow wine, is the second most popular wine and made with grains, wheat, or some other grain. And *mijiu*, or rice wine, is the most traditional of the three and also found in Japan and Korea.

I managed to get some good value *baijiu*, which should possess one of five different tastes or sensations. This *baijiu* should be the deep taste sensation if I didn't buy incorrectly.

A knock on the classic Chinese wooden door. I hurry to it, having just come out of the steamy hot shower with nothing but the plush, bleached white hotel bathrobe.

I open it. Miao Miao enters with an elegant, black dress.

"That's a different change from last time," I note.

I turn on a bit of Spotify for some modern sensual music with a heavy downbeat. I open the *bajiiu* and pour each of us a small dose.

"*Gan bei*," I say in native Mandarin. Cheers.

We knock our glasses and down the mini shot.

It's warm, but not burning, like a trail of liquid gold going down

the throat.

Delicious.

* * *

After a few shots, we relax on the couch together and she looks into my eyes as we are talking.

We didn't get to talk much last time. And this time around, I notice many more things. More things than just pussy eating.

Like her hair. It's slick back, cute, nice. Long hair, which she now wears in a bun, highlighting her neck.

Her choice of dress. She doesn't have the most curvy figure, so she chose a sleek, silk dress that flows down to her ankles.

And then her heels, from the silver, sparkling fastener that winds down from her ankles and highlights her straight long legs, calves, and toes.

We talk about life. What she likes to do on the weekend. How her life is.

This is what's great. To connect.

Sure I like fucking like every guy, but it's better to connect first. Way better.

I move closer. I kiss her.

14

I can tell our sexual energy is compatible.

* * *

I undress her by grasping the dress' two shoulder straps and just slipping it past her shoulders.

Her dress falls to the slightly course carpet. Just like in Bruno Mars' *Versace on the Floor.*

Miao Miao stands before me in all-black *Agent Provocateur* lingerie.

First, her panties. With a black thong, sheer tulle, with floral embroidery and a cute pink satin bow.

Her matching bra, with the same embroidery and bow, and gold-toned sliders on the straps.

"Delicious," I mutter to myself.

I push her gently to the bed. She falls gently, lying flat now.

I unbutton the flap in the lingerie that opens access to her pussy.

Her pussy was so delicious last time I had to have that first today.

"Well, hello again," I say, as I greet the shaved kitty.

Miao Miao giggles.

I start licking her first, remembering that she liked my licking motion from the bottom of the pussy towards the top. I do that a few times, keen to get her started.

Miao Miao starts settling in.

This time, she starts getting wet quickly. I play with her kitty some more, flicking the clit for good measure.

Miao Miao lets out a small moan.

Seeing her beginning wetness, I lick my middle finger. I slowly, very slowly, enter that finger into her vagina.

Miao Miao lets out another moan, this time a little louder.

I finger fuck her, starting slowly, feeling out the insides of her pussy. It's super wet, allowing me easy access, my middle finger sloshing about.

Sensing my opportunity, I withdraw and enter her again with two fingers, increasing the girth penetrating her.

"Yesssss, like that," she sighs.

I put my hand on her mound, now making a circular motion on her clit.

I start increasing the speed of my rotation as my fingers continue to go in and out of her. They crescendo at a nice pace, both stimulating her vagina and clit.

"Ooooh...I'm cumming," she moans.

I love her moans once I start fingering her. She moans so satisfyingly, so deeply, so horny. As if she feels it and doesn't care if anyone hears it.

There are moaners and screamers. I love them both, but am partial to the moaners. They just sound more real.

But I don't mind the other either.

I continue to massage Miao Miao's cootch, increasing the rhythm now and reaching deeper into her pussy. I take my hand away from her clit every so often, kissing and licking her instead, but always keeping my two fingers inside her.

To feel my size.

Miao Miao claws my arms and thrusts her hips at me as I change up the tempo. More as I increase the rhythm.

She's totally into it now. Her hips move toward me whenever I thrust.

"I'm cumming.... ahh....," she screams, as her body shakes and convulses.

I take my sloppy fingers out of her sloppy vagina, satisfied with my work. I lick my fingers in front of her, wanting her to see.

That turns her on.

She flips up, looks into my eyes, and pushes me down on my chest.

Without breaking eye contact, she grabs my cock with her hand and extends her tongue out of her mouth.

"You want me?" Miao Miao teases.

I nod. Just a bit. Not too easy to please, you know.

She starts bobbing on my cock. She's slurping and slopping, and teasing.

I love the sounds that she makes.

I hold her hair as she deepthroats my cock. She really wants to satisfy me for all the cumming I gave her, cupping my balls gently to double the pleasure.

"You like to eat my cock, you dirty slut?" I ask.

She responds by further deep-throating my cock.

She likes dirty talk. Great.

"Come and eat daddy. Make daddy feel good," I continue.

She continues bobbing up and down, my cock disappearing into her gorgeous mouth.

I love the sounds she's making. Those sounds make all the

difference from a good cock sucker or not. The desire to not only physically satisfy, but to visually and audibly satisfy.

It all feels so good. But it's been a bit too long since I had a taste of that sweet pussy.

I want some now.

I guide her up, her now in front of me with her perky dark tits. I weasel my way between her legs as if I'm going into a foxhole upside down.

"Continue, my dear," I say to Miao Miao, "if you can."

I enjoy my buffet, savouring her now sweet sex with the right viscosity of her pussy juices. Combined with my saliva and my tongue darting inside her.

How I enjoy parting her pussy lips. Those sweet things, begging for me to suck.

She's eating me, I eating her. Both trying to satisfy each other with fury.

"Ooooh," she coos, enjoying it and taking her mouth off my cock.

That's a penalty, I note. She stopped first.

I push her ass forward to my cock, rotating her as she goes.

"Ride me," I say simply.

She grabs my cock and puts me inside her. I love that feeling when a woman does that. Takes charge and puts it inside her.

She grinds on top of me.

I see her perky tits in front, bouncing up and down, her hair flying up and down to match the rhythm.

We start to sweat. I notice a hint of sweat now beading, my full body feeling the sensation of sweat and sex.

It feels like sport now, fucking. Not making love, not seduction.

Just raw fucking. And I love it.

As she smashes on top of me, I match her thrust by pushing my pelvis deep inside her, as if the combined slap would harden my cock and go further into her pussy.

And apparently it does, as Miao Miao leans her head back, her hair falling back, her eyes looking straight into the sky. Her sweat beads start to secrete near her neck as she looks for a bit of respite.

No luck. I'm not giving it to her.

I quicken my pace, thrusting my tool vertically inside her. My two hands cup her breasts, squeezing them, adding to the friction and the heat generated, my sweat mixing with her.

"Ugh ugh ugh," she pants, enjoying our union, our fucking.

Her skin glistens as the full moon's light enters the room and reflects off it. Miao Miao lives in the moment owning her pleasure, my cock occupying a space inside her body, and my masculine energy enthralling her entire being.

3

The Tasting Menu

Panda tells me to bring some red wine today.

I wasn't quite sure what to make of it, as is normal during these surreptitious Telegram conversations. Panda also tells me that there would be a new lady.

I put the two and two together that the red wine is going to help put the new lady at ease.

As a Gentleman, I aim to please.

My sleep has been just ok since I arrived at Narita Airport in Tokyo from San Francisco. I have a bit of jet lag, spending restless nights at the Hyatt in Roppongi, me sometimes going downstairs for a walk in the Hills to get my mind off things. My mind had been racing quite a bit since we need to get our metrics right for our next fundraising round.

Suffice to say, I was worried I wouldn't have much time to pick

up the bottle of wine either.

Right before the soiree I manage to head to an international supermarket about 10 minutes from *Azabu-jiuban* to pick up the beverage. As an experienced wine drinker, I do know my stuff and peruse the aisles for the right red, something with a bold compelling label, but interesting flavour and profile.

I go through the normal stuff. Some Hardy's, some Penfolds.

I personally like a bold red like a Cabernet Sauvignon, but I know ladies like Merlots or Shirazes.

A Cabernet has a bold profile, a thick, syrupy taste, bold in flavours and palette. It's like a woman with thick breasts and hips in a red dress, attracting all the men's eyes with her boldness and holding on to that attention through the subtle curves of the fabric and voluptuous feminine shape.

Merlot, on the other hand, is a more seductive wine. Like a slightly slimmer woman with a dark dress, the fabric not immediately drawing a man's eye but leaving something to the imagination with a long slit in the back, tempting a man to explore her secrets.

And then there's Rioja. An easy-to-drink wine, like a casual cute girl, easy to drink and easy on the eyes. Something you can savour almost every day and never get bored.

Those are my usuals. But today is not a usual night with the new girl, who I want to impress with my wine selection.

I find a Shiraz that has a modern art label that Rothko would be proud of. It calls itself a Barossa Ink.

I am intrigued. I know Barossa Valley in Australia, but the way it describes itself is appealing. "An intense and opulent wine", but a Shiraz.

I buy it.

I stroll back to the Hyatt in Roppongi, with a quick pace as I am a bit late. I also have some more work to do later tonight, which I aim to finish quickly.

Luckily, I have booked my room in the same hotel as the party. But Panda doesn't know that.

I ping Panda in advance, saying that I am at the lobby even before I am there. I have to recover a bit of time.

I see Panda.

She gives me the keys as they brush my Rolex oyster bracelet, shooshing me to head up myself first. Room 603.

I think this is quite strange as she usually comes up with me. But I'm on the clock and decide to heed her directions and head up myself.

So there are two rooms for tonight's arrangement, and when I arrive one is full and the other not so. As my normal self I am rather shy, electing to take my shower and clean up first.

I had seen a few members in the lobby waiting to come up as well, but to avoid any awkward mistakes, I didn't look directly at them. Better to be surprised later than to say something and break the ice with someone not from the party.

Not very cool to assume someone is a member of a sex party when they're just in the hotel lobby waiting for their granny.

I take my shower. I open up the Barossa Shiraz as others shower as well. It is a great and fantastic way to unwind.

I still have some work to do so I dutifully finish it on my laptop, grabbing a quiet corner in the quiet massage room.

I start to hear a woman called Bean's soft moans in the other room. She seems to be getting satisfaction from a cock that is filling her, from the sounds of her moans.

It's great for her to start the night's festivities. Her groans set the mood for all, foreshadowing tonight's hedonism.

The other room, the massage room I'm currently in, is with Miao Miao receiving some 1 on 1 attention and a new girl Summer getting a 6 hand massage. Or 8.

I can't tell she is getting so much attention.

I put down my laptop. I start slowly and watch a bit first, with the girl in the other room being pounded conservatively, Miao Miao getting her massage and a slight pussy rub, and Summer getting a normal massage-cum-fingering with her perky ass

lifted in the air.

We were previously told that Miao Miao and Summer would not be having sex tonight. But we all hoped that it wasn't true.

Or at least, I hoped it wasn't true.

The cacophony of sex continues, crescendoing with every moan, every cock or finger in a pussy, every cock that the ladies are warmly stroking in their luscious, full mouths.

I can't resist. No, I don't want to resist.

I am horny.

* * *

I jump in.

I first exercise my cock in Bean's mouth as I finger her thick, pussy lips, enveloped by her curly pubes.

Her voluptuous body writhes with pleasure, her large breasts wriggling, her legs splayed apart to welcome my circling fingers.

She sucks hard, trying as she can to get me hard, knowing that my thick, pulsing well-shaved cock is about to pleasure her. She sucks with delight, soft and light, like a light vacuum playing with my pulsing throb.

I love it when a girl pulls me in.

I thrust my cock further into her mouth, testing her limit and how much she can take in. And she takes it all in, tenderly.

Time for me to assert myself.

"Turn over," I strongly suggest, pulling her ass to the edge of the bed, her standing up and her elbows resting on the bed.

Her pussy and her ass lay in front of me, those thick pussy lips ready for me to thrust in.

I thrust my throb inside her, doggy style.

She gasps at the suddenness. A moan.

I start slow on her pussy, me doing my rhythmic ins and outs. Her moans match my rhythm, her pussy warmly wrapping around my cock like a warm, comfortable mouth.

Not too tight though. Just enough.

I want to hear her moan more. I love it when a girl gives verbal feedback.

I quicken my pace. I hear my balls slap her clit with each stroke. I make sure that each stroke does that, reminding her that I am behind, stimulating her in multiple ways.

Boom. Boom. Boom. I thrust like a man. No, an animal, my cock wanting to break her apart, boldened by my balls adding to the percussion.

"Take it," I command. I feel my cock base at the edge of her ass, my fullness entirely inside Bean.

"Ugghhhh," she moans, a guttural sound.

I withdraw. Bean collapses onto the bed.

"Never want to cum too soon," I remind myself, "You have plenty to do tonight."

* * *

I graduate over to the next room and Miao Miao. I help massage her, as a Gentleman should.

Miao Miao's body, thin with her usual perky tits, lies face down, a total contrast to Bean's full figure. She welcomes my warm touch as I stroke her tired shoulders and neck muscles.

"Is this good," I ask, as I stroke harder and firmer along the muscle lines, each stroke increasing in depth and intensity.

"Mmmm," she responds, as she melts into the rhythm of my strokes, each manoeuvre seemingly both soothing her tired muscles and increasing her basic desires.

Like a good boy, I only seek to pleasure.

Not this time. She suddenly flips over, exposing her now dark, perky nipples in their glory, eager to display her appreciation of my hard work. She rewards me with an eager, hungry look.

"I want to taste your full cock"

She swallows my warmth full, her eyes closing eagerly, concerned with one task and one task only.

My pleasure.

Her thin lips envelop my cock, her warm mouth and tongue tickling my shaft. She sucks with fury, with eagerness.

I continue her energy, grabbing her manicured fingers and thrusting them towards my ball sack. I want her to play with my balls, which she, like a good girl, obeys.

She does one further.

She reaches further still, grabbing my ass, pulling my hips and cock deeper into her mouth.

The tip of my cock feels the back of her throat, my shaft fully enveloped and warm, her pursed lips applying just enough pressure as if a warm, tight pussy.

I nearly cum.

I withdraw. "Girl, can I fuck you?"

"No," she says, "my doctor said I can't."

"Hmph," I say, feigning anger, eager to violate her today.

"I want your cock," she explains, "I so badly want it. But..."

"Say no more," I say, "there's always next time".

I so want to fuck her, but it's never too good to be persistent or needy. There is always a next time.

* * *

There is now the new girl Summer, warmed up, now being fingered and fucked in all directions. The previously shy girl that came into the hotel, with her hair neatly in a bun and bling Donna Karen watch, is now a wild nymph taking in cocks in all directions.

Her D-cups are full on her slim figure, her cute belly ring and cursive writing on her shoulder tattoo marking her body, her small hands cute whilst taking in the large cocks around her.

I love a good girl gone slutty.

I eagerly join in the action, thrusting my warmth into her mouth, taking the only non-occupied pleasuring space left.

She takes my cock in her mouth and swallows me whole.

I open up my legs, kneeling on one and opening the other, straddling her face so she would have open access to my cock, balls, and ass.

She grabs my ass, thrusting me inside her warm, sweet mouth.

I moan.

She is good. Too good. She is naughty, I can see it in her eyes.

I mouth fuck her some more, but I have to rest a bit lest I cum right then.

I withdraw. I pull her ass to the edge of the bed, her standing up.

I want to hear her moan. She is still stopping herself, self-conscious as this is her first time, not wanting to let herself go.

I want her. I want to mark her. To have her scream, to demand my cock. To desire me.

I thrust my cock inside her. I pump my manliness inside.

I can see her manicured and coloured toes curl up. I grab her hands and pull her back, her back arching up, my cock pushing deeper and higher into her pussy. I love that feeling.

She seems to as well. I can see her back muscles tense, her skin glistening with a slight sweat.

I taste her skin. Oh, it is sweet. Like a macaron, with just enough sweet and salty.

I bite her on her back, wanting to leave a private, small mark to claim her.

I withdraw quickly. I want to carry on with my tasting, wanting to taste her pussy.

Her pussy lips are thin, not as thick as Panda's, and not as thin as Miao Miao's.

Like the Goldilocks' rule. Just right.

I push my tongue in, like a mini cock, for that taste.

Slightly sweet, but neutral. But wow, it is incredibly yummy.

I want some more.

I tongue fuck her, making sure that the tip of my tongue is hitting her clit first, then thrusting my base into her whole vagina.

It tastes even better inside.

She moans.

"A girl that appreciates being eaten," I say to myself, "make sure to keep satisfying her."

I am going to ravage Summer tonight. She is everything, everything I want tonight.

I was consumed with desire. But now I am ignited with fire, the fire of my lust.

I wet my fingers with my mouth and put my two fingers in her hole. Deep. So deep I can feel her vagina walls, raw from all the fucking tonight, but wet in anticipation for more.

I finger fuck her, changing and flipping my hand over every so often, making sure I hit her clit button along with my thrusts, me wanting to hit her G spot too.

I want it all with Summer. To fuck her in every which way. She is mine tonight.

She moans. Louder now, a throaty type of moan. Her inhibitions now forgotten, a primal type of tone, ready for an animal to do whatever he pleases with her.

I want more. I want her passion, her primal passion, for her to lose control of herself.

My engorgement, now full alert, is ready. I direct it into her smooth, sweet pussy, filling her inside.

She moans again, but now slightly softer. She is consumed with her own passion, without knowing what else is happening around her, engulfed in waves of passion and sex, lost in pleasure.

My cock thrusts repeatedly inside her. Whilst I finger her clit, my other hand grabs her D-cups. I whisper in her ears, demanding she take it like a good girl.

I can see her coloured toes curl up again, eager for my cock to hit

her G spot at the right angle, her adjusting to suit her pleasure.

She wants her pleasure. What is hers. And I am giving her that.

I pump her from behind, quickening my pace now, eager to cum inside her, wanting my pleasure to come from her.

I can feel my balls slapping her clit, clip clap, with a rhythm of a battering ram, keen to penetrate deeper each stroke, each time.

I am coming. My pleasure overwhelms me, my usual restrained self succumbing to the waves of ecstasy that only a moment ago engulfed Summer.

I cum, wave after wave. Summer drives her hips into my cock, eager to squeeze out each and last drop of passion, until I am no more.

"Good god," I sigh, "you are good."

* * *

We all leave around 10:15 PM. It is time well spent. A bit of everything, something new, something old.

I go back to Summer as I get dressed. She is just out of the shower, with droplets on her smooth, sweet skin.

I give her a hug, an American full-body style and not European.

"Thank you," I say. In English.

She looks deeply into my eyes, her small hands holding mine, her late to let go, slowly releasing my fingers one by one.

"I'll see you next time?" I whisper.

She nods. Gently, innocently, Summer back to her normal, demure self.

I am happy. I helped welcome her to the club. As a Gentleman should.

4

A Sparkling Shiraz

For this session, Panda suggests a wine that is just casual.

Casual can be boring, however.

The art is in turning the casual to something sensual.

I'm walking around in Wan Chai, Hong Kong, thinking about somewhere to buy some wine for tonight's event. I'm in town on a long layover, heading to other parts of Asia as part of our fundraise.

I find a nondescript supermarket in the middle of Wan Chai that purveys only Australian goods, like the usual meats and reds that the country is known for. As a lark, I decide to walk in.

I ask for something interesting from the staff. As expected, they don't respond with anything that I think is interesting. Just things that are on sale.

I'm after something you don't normally see. That you think is quite normal and boring, but it's not.

Just like what I hope for tonight.

Suddenly – I find it. Nestled between the bosoms of the shiraz and the pinot noir.

Sparking shiraz.

Interesting, I think. I've never heard of the two together.

I imagine what it would be like. The depth of a shiraz, but the bubbles of a champagne? Of a cremant? Probably not as fine, but would it be good enough? Or disappointing like American bastard wines?

A good wine helps a woman's desire open up. It unhinges the shackles of propriety, frees the carnal, and accentuates the sexual energy.

Get it right, and the night becomes right.

* * *

I walk into the hotel, the Mandarin Oriental in Hong Kong. The old one, not the new one.

The old ways are sometimes the best. Just like my Gieves & Hawkes jacket tonight, which I inherited from my father.

I walk up the marble stone steps, next to the Captain's Bar, and head straight to the elevators next to the small boutique.

I always find that small boutique quite charming, purveying old tactile goods like newspapers and magazines. Things that you can touch, feel, and smell.

I go up. There are 2 other guys already.

"This is going to be a rather small affair," I think to myself.

We do a bit of small talk while I open up the wine and have a drink. I like to savour my wines, so this gives me a chance to taste it first before serving it to others.

It is yum again. The bright bubbles of a champagne, with the pinky colour and deep tones of a shiraz.

Perhaps a richer blanc de noir would be a worthy comparison.

A knock on the door.

In comes Jas.

A short girl, with a thick body and pointed face, very well put together. Her equally thick full breasts nestled inside her busty bra, the tension ready to be released in a few moments.

In contrast, her black short skirt shows her bare legs, drawing the eye upwards from calf to crotch, leaving something, something naughty and salacious, to the imagination.

She appears as if she came from a lunch date with family, or something formal. Not overly formal as in business, but well put together casually.

I like a girl that's well put together on the outside. It makes the anticipation of what's underneath that immaculate outside more fun.

To want to break that shell. A challenge to unlock and enjoy each others' sexual energy.

She sits down. I pour her some wine.

Jas is immediately anti-establishment. She talks about life and mainly education. About how education standards are degrading, how they don't train young people to think, that they are all sheep.

Oof. So direct.

I'm not usually that up front, preferring first to see how people act, how people think. Observe the surroundings first.

Read the room, as they say. You know, never talk about sex, politics, and religion in polite conversation. Especially when in a room with strangers.

I go along though. "Tell me more," I say.

And you know what - her spark starts to turn me on. Her directness. Her lack of propriety. Of social norms.

You can tell a lot about how someone fucks by how they speak. How they think. How they act.

My attention, in return, turns her on.

She now looks into my eyes as we speak, intimate with my very words, my thoughts, my intentions.

I am almost embarrassed by how much attention she gives me. Her eagerness. Her attention. Her desire.

No, not desire. Need. To fuck.

* * *

I undress Jas, slowly, Miss Dior enveloping me as I unbutton her blouse, button by button.

The release of the tension, the tug of the button as it escapes from its hole, the fabric springing and vibrating back to its original shape.

Underneath that prim outfit is indeed that voluminous body, decorated with a black, lacy one-piece lingerie.

Then it is the black mini skirt's turn.

One button. One zip. The lingerie lines continue down, teasing the eyes as they lead me down to her crotch, now open and free are her thick, juicy, pussy lips.

Juicy indeed, like an oyster waiting to be devoured, with my tongue wanting to probe to find the pearl.

I dig in.

My tongue tenderly touches the bottom of her vagina, where the vagina and the perineum meet, cleanly shaven for tonight's festivities. I lap up, from there to the clit, ensuring that I don't penetrate, but that the flat, large, wide base of my tongue separates her labia lips, like parting a sea of sex.

I repeat again, like a good boy, savouring her sweet vagina and the slightly sweet sex starting to secrete. I pleasure her again with my tongue, upwards, parting those thick labia lips, ending with a bit of a flick of the tongue on the clit now.

She shudders.

I now repeat the same motion but penetrate her vagina with the tip of my tongue, going straight into her tasty pinky vaginal walls, the flat, wide, base of my tongue still moving upwards, parting the labia lips fully now as I go.

Slowly though. Of course slowly. Tantalisingly slowly, as if to explore her every part and every taste.

A cooch tasting.

Her clit reveals itself from its hood, emboldened with desire, wanting a bit of the action.

I comply, now moving upwards after my last lap, pursing my lips as I tease the clit with little sounds of suction.

She loves it.

She drives her mound toward my mouth, her direct moans making sure I know the extent of her pleasure. Meanwhile, the other guys keep her busy, one flanking her with his cock in her hand, the other with his manhood in her mouth.

Jas likes to be a busy girl.

She toys with one boy's cock with her one hand, pleasuring his tool, her manicured nails adding some decorative colour to the flesh. Wrapping her fingertips around the tip of his cock, then enveloping her hand quickly around his crown, aided by the gliding lube, she slides down his shaft, fully, wholly, and to the base of his balls.

Each thrust of her hand turns his cock darker in colour, the lube glistening off his cock and revealing its beautiful curve, quivering as it anticipates the next pleasure.

Her mouth and tongue equally busy, her eyes and long lashes closed, she sucks off another man's dick, all 8 inches of him, deep-throating him to his base.

The other man's cock pushes the insides of her cheeks, her tongue wrapping around his tool, the tightness of her mouth rivalling any tight warm pussy.

She slurps with delight, knowing that each motion and sound not only pleasures him physically, but heightens his sensation, hearing his manhood being satisfied and pleasured.

And I? I have the pleasure of eating pussy, which I much wanted to do today, searching for that pearl.

I suck her clit, but penetrate her with two curved fingers, hitting the fleshy, lumpy spot at the front of her vagina.

My fingers are moist going in as I hear the slishing and sloshing of them exploring her hole.

Her G spot engorges, the vaginal wall more prominent, more sensitive, more open to my fingering charms.

I know I've got it right. Oh, I know.

Jas starts to climax, grabbing my arm with her one free hand as she struggles to get words out.

"Fuck," she moans, the precise word not coming quite out with a full cock in her mouth.

I hear her throat gag as the other man continues to thrust his cock inside her mouth, keen to get everything in.

And like a good girl, she takes it all in.

I love the half moan, half gag. Jas is fighting against her survival instinct for her to let her primal urge out, to let me know what

feels good.

The more pleasure I give her, the more she wants to reciprocate the pleasure to others. As if she was giving into her pleasure, and now channelling her feminine energy to give pleasure to others, increasingly more as her pleasure increases.

My throb quivers. I am turned on even more.

At this point, I am starting to get slightly jealous. My poor cock is not getting satisfied.

I am giving pleasure, but alas, I am not a recipient.

I look up at Jas. She is continuing to pleasure the other men, one hand stroking, her mouth doing. The others are having a great time from the sounds of it.

She looks at me, devilishly directly in my eyes.

"Do you want me?" she looks at me sluttily as if to say "Do you want your cock to get some too?"

Now's my turn.

I flip her over, pushing out the other guys.

My cock will get satisfied now, damnit. 69 style.

I insert my cock in her well-worked mouth, pushing myself into it like a well-lubed pussy, making sure she takes in everything.

For all the cock pleasuring the other guys get, but none for me.

With vigour and anger I keep searching for that precious pearl, sometimes sucking, sometimes fingering. I am a man on a mission there, slurping with delight, my spit mixing with her pussy juices, a dangerous cocktail of sex.

Those thick labia lips are so good, little pockets of lust for me to suck on, to keep me busy.

I leave no stone unturned. No crevasse unpleasured.

Equally, I love filling her mouth with my cock and having her reward me. Her tongue is so good and warm.

It feels so good. It belongs there.

* * *

We're sitting on the couch. Taking a break from the play before.

Sipping the sparkling shiraz, the bubbles still a joyous mouthful, tickling the tongue and the throat as it goes down.

We continue our conversation, which has now moved to living in Hong Kong. How she enjoys the quality of life, how the food is great, the wines are good.

I nod patiently, not to elevate the conversation, but to continue moving it along.

I have an agenda now. My pleasure.

She notices.

Perhaps it's my nodding. Perhaps by my not-so-subtle leaning into her, my arm leaning against her back towards my manhood.

Jas' thick lips come over and start playing with my flaccid cock, getting me hard.

My soldier doesn't take long to spring into action, livening up quickly as I feel it increasing in length and girth right in Jas' mouth.

I feel strong and confident as Jas has to make more room in her for me. I challenge her to take me all in, all the way to my base.

Her mass of long, jet-black hair in front of me, bobbing up and down. Her gaggle pulsates the air, once populated with the noise of active conversation, now only the noise of active hedonism.

I tie her hair back with my right hand, freeing her to do her best work, and to observe her beautiful face and mouth solely devoted to my pleasure.

I watch her pleasure me eagerly, mixing tongue and teeth, slurping and sucking, driving and dipping.

"Good girl," I coo, "good girl. Do it to Daddy."

I ask quickly, "Do you swallow?" Politely of course.

It wasn't a no.

In fact she doesn't give a response, continuing to suck like the devil, like the slut that she is.

I take the lead. Now's my turn to own my pleasure, to feel good.

I shoot my shot.

I'm naughty. Too bad.

Her slutty eyes look at me as I cum, half surprised, half impressed that I impose my will, my right to my pleasure.

Her thick, luscious lips reward my throbbing cock, squeezing every drop, my ejaculate warming her entire mouth, her capturing my manhood inside and not letting go.

Wave after wave of warmth explode inside her, hitting her tongue, the roof, the tonsils.

I let it all go.

I feel my balls squeezing towards my body as if coordinating with each and every suck from Jas, as she delightfully honours each drop.

Her eyes continue to look into mine as she keeps me inside her mouth, speaking to me as if to say "Am I good girl?" I feel the slight suction as she opens her throat to swallow it all in.

Seeing that I like that feeling, she continues to have my cock inside, sucking all my cum, her cheeks now taut to take it all in whilst looking deeply from her slutty eyes into mine.

It is the best blowjob I've had in a while. She is a darling.

Her special treat for me.

5

Two Sojus

Panda tells me there are going to be two girls, but doesn't tell me who.

What a tease.

She, like usual, says it will be a casual affair. Just some light drinks will do, she says.

I'm in Seoul this trip, as part of our Asian fundraising tour before I head back to the Bay Area. I really don't like to fly into Seoul. It's too tough to get into the city, the Airport Limousine bus taking 2 hours to get into the city.

I head to a *conveni*, a convenience store, to get some drinks. I pick up a few cheap *Chamisul sojus*.

I walk back to the hotel, the Westin in *Cheongdamdong*. One of my favourite hotels in the city. It overlooks the market and has a wonderful buffet.

49

I've heard the pool is nice too, but I haven't been in a while.

I head up to the 20th floor.

There's just me. The girls are late.

I decide to take a shower first, as I always do, liking to relax and grab a quick shot or two of the *soju*s to unwind. I'm careful to hang my Anderson & Sheppard jacket and put my Rolex GMT to the side.

I wonder who will be coming today?

* * *

Ah. Panda has arranged some of my favourite girls. Very nice of her.

Jas and Bean.

Jas I've had before. Bean, also.

I love them both.

Women who just like to have sex. I've played with them before and it's an absolute joy.

People who know sex know that it doesn't matter what the girl is like. Whether she is big or small, thin or thick. As the man, you have to figure out what the girl is like and try to satisfy her.

In this, and in many things, women come first.

Jas, who has arrived first, decides to get me hard first.

She unpacks my tool gently, pulling down my underwear and warming it with her gentle fingers. She opens her mouth, further warming my cock as it smoothly enters her mouth.

My cock tip shudders as it hits her tongue, sensitive to the touch, to the curling of her wet, slippery tongue as it wraps around my shaft.

Her warm mouth continues to wrap around my tool, warming the entirety of my shaft, covering it with a thin coat of wet saliva.

Her lips apply pressure, gently cupping my cock. I feel the fullness of her lips.

Her suction, coupled with her saliva and her tongue, creates the beginning of the pleasure of the night.

I withdraw my engorged cock from Jas' warm receptacle and I push her towards the bed forcefully.

She falls back, her ass landing on the bed, her head landing on the pillows, her legs flying upwards.

In one motion, I swoop in with my cock honed in towards Jas' pussy, my hands cradling her legs by the back of her knees.

I plunge deeply into her. My penis, lubricated with a mix of her

saliva and sex, smoothly enters her all the way to the depths of her pussy and the base of my lingham.

Without hesitation, I rhythmically continue, my hips driving into her, my cock as if on auto drive and with a mind of its own fulfilling its purpose.

"Ooh," she coos, "give it to meeee."

I flip Jas over. I want to feel her from behind.

Bean appears, as if on cue, naked. She lies herself down on the bed, pushing her mound towards Jas' mouth as I enter her from behind.

"That's a great start," I say to myself.

* * *

I continue to push myself into Jas from behind, my cock disappearing into her hole as if a disappearing trick.

Jas moans, but quickly goes back to eating Bean out, with Bean looking directly in my eyes as her pussy is being pleasured.

I tell Bean to flip over, doggy style as well. I want to penetrate both at the same time.

I push my cock deep into Bean now, her pussy looser, smoother, deeper.

She moans, with a deeper baritone voice, "oooohhhhh."

I withdraw, pushing myself into Jas. Her pussy is much tighter, my cock feeling every little bit, every little inch of her vagina.

Jas moans, "Ahhhhh", with a higher school girl pitch.

I go at the two girls one at a time, like a metronome, tick tock, tick tock. They are looking at each other, kissing and making out between their different-pitched moans, both getting stimulated by me, their pussy juices being mixed on the slippery shaft of my cock.

I pause.

I stay inside Jas, my cock filling her entire pussy. I insert my left hand inside Bean's vagina, all the way to the hilt.

I fuck both of them together, their moans lighting up the room, their energy adding to the atmosphere.

It's awesome.

Now I want both girls, now face up. I command them to turn over.

I repeat the same as before. My cock in Jas, then my cock in Bean.

Bean and Jas kiss, their moans and souls lost in each others' pleasure, their saliva mixed by their own accord, their sex mixed

by my cock inside them.

Their pale bodies writhing in pleasure, their hands touching each other, 2 pairs of breasts looking at me, wriggling, shaking with every thrust, every pleasure.

I love doing both of the girls, sometimes Bean, sometimes Jas, getting them inside and deep, my cock tip pushing their G spot.

It's a feast for all my senses, their senses, our senses.

The sounds, the sights, the pleasure my cock and their pussies receive, crescendoing into the Seoul night, a sacred sensory symphony of sex.

6

The Bubbly

Panda says tonight will be a special experience. "A model!" she types excitedly.

"Great," I type back on Telegram, our normal mode of communication. "I've always wanted to play with a model."

"...and her husband the photographer."

"Um. What?"

Do I get to fuck the model, whilst her husband is looking? Would I be able to get hard? What would the husband do?

I spend the whole day thinking about this one, even during meetings with our technology partners. Sure I am excited, but also a bit unsettled.

I go downstairs mid-day to a Taipei supermarket in my Huntsman tailored suit, looking for something for tonight's soiree.

Something refreshing, light. Appropriate for a model.

The issue with Taipei supermarkets is that the selection is not that good. There are not that many small vineyard wines, only the big brands, like Penfolds, Krug, Veuve Clicquot.

Champagne. That's it.

After all, there are no calories in champagne. And the bubbles make it easier for everyone to get drunk easily.

Especially for me.

* * *

I arrive at the W.

It's a beautiful lobby, wide open space, with good looking people going in and out. I hear the W is THE place to stay in Taipei, as it is popular for the rich kids of Taipei to head there and party.

I look forward to tonight's good-looking people. I head upstairs to our room.

I am introduced to the husband first. Half. He seems nice, with bohemian brown hair, dark John Lennon sunglasses, his Leica M11 nestled around his neck.

"Very photographer-like," I say to myself.

"Nice to meet you," he offers, probably knowing that I'm the

interloper here.

I am introduced to Sandra.

I mutter under my breath, "hot."

Strong jawline but feminine. Her makeup is done right, not too heavy, but with the right touches to accentuate her eyes and her thick, gorgeous lips.

And her body, which I follow along with the curves of her jeans and her crop top. They're flowing and cresting in the right places.

But it's her hair that sticks out. Full and lively, with nice curves. It has volume, it looks gorgeous. It looks like she's put some time in, heading to the salon, getting it blown dry, getting some product thrown in for it to hold.

I quickly move on to the champagne before I get too distracted by my imagination.

I pop the bottle of the yellow labelled Veuve, surprising Sandra slightly. The bubbles leak out from the top, like a bit of pre cum from the tip of a cock.

"Ohh," she giggles, "I like bubbles!"

"This is going to be fun," I think to myself.

* * *

We get started.

Sandra disrobes, her just-showered body now glistening, revealing her curved figure. She's got all the proportions of a model, tall and lengthy legs, with a size B cup. Her skin and figure are flawless.

But it's her still-perfect bob that makes me notice. Those perfect curves and layers. I've never seen anything like it.

Sandra starts modelling.

"Is this what I need to do?" she asks Half as she starts posing, as she looks for affirmation.

She has the energy of a cute girl. She asks for validation, questions on what looks good for the camera, her body to be commanded.

Half takes the lead, his Leica flipping vertically and horizontally.

"Move this way," he barks, "put your ass here!"

Sandra complies, shifting her ass from the edge to the centre of the bed. She sits down, pulling her knees to her chest.

Half barks further. "Move your tits up a bit," he directs.

Sandra does so willingly.

So she is cute. Up to a point.

Sandra starts to settle in, and as she does so, she starts to model. She crosses her legs in a feminine way, scissors her legs to draw the eye towards her mound, only to cover it up slightly, leaving the mind to desire.

Half doesn't speak anymore, letting Sandra to do her work. Thank God.

She crosses her arms across her chest, pushing her breasts up, cupping her perky tits.

Sandra draws the attention now to her face, putting her finger suggestively near the corners of her mouth, the finger tips not quite penetrative, touching the corner just slightly.

Suddenly, Sandra flips over on the bed, her ass in the air, her fingers in her mouth, awakening her desire.

Her perky ass lifts up. Ready to take a cock in, her tight ass air fucking an invisible shaft.

I notice a palatable change in her energy, from just going through the motions of modelling to now going through the motions of seduction.

She no longer has the idea of attracting a man, a physical person, but is trying to court desire herself.

She spreads her legs while bending over, inserting her own fingers inside. Her arm between her legs, her face lying flat on the bed, her beautiful hair splayed across, sexily, alive.

"Yes," she moans, "mmmmm."

Her moans are full of desire. Of carnal pleasure.

She puts herself further in, her sounds with seriousness, ferociousness, hunger. I see her manicured nails disappearing into her hole, hear her fingers going inside and out, the moisture amplifying the sounds.

"Yaaassss," she gasps, "ummmm."

Half takes pictures, he increasing the pace, the shutter going off, quickening.

He circles her from the front to the back, capturing her heightening pleasure.

She keeps on fingering herself. Moaning. Wanting. Biting.

"I'm cumming!!" she moans, her fingers fucking ferociously.

I am hard. The energy in the room, her carnal pleasures, all make me fucking horny.

Half senses the same, putting the Leica down and taking off his shirt. It is time.

Sandra lifts her just fucked hair, her eyes with a daze of desire. She looks directly at me.

"No, Half," Sandra says, "I want the Gentleman."

* * *

She slithers like a serpent of sex, towards me, towards my cock. Her eyes aggressive.

I, my apprehension present but courage reinforced by bubbly, with my soldier standing tall, ready to do its duty that his master is not ready for.

With her hungry eyes, she opens her mouth, begging for my cock to fill her mouth, her eyes saying "let me taste your cock and pre-cum."

She takes my full cock, putting her thick full lips all over it.

"Mmmm," she purrs, "that's a big boy!" My warmth pushes her mouth to the limit.

Sandra goes to town with delight, sucking and slurping, looking sexily into my eyes.

I grab the champagne. "Open wide," I growl, dripping the Veuve down her throat. Sandra sticks out her tongue to catch the drops like she will with my cum.

I drip the Veuve over her body and lick it off. At the same time, I penetrate her with my fingers, what she did to herself a minute ago.

"Oooooh," she gasps, taking in all my fingers, "put it all inside!"

Her pussy increases its desire, getting more moist and welcoming my two fingers in.

Half is behind me, I hear him clicking away on his Leica. And there's nothing he can do about it but watch me about to fuck his wife.

"Fuck me hard," she half gasps, half begs, "fuck me now!"

I insert myself in her well-lubed pussy, my cock thirsty for her now. It seems even stiffer and harder, eager to do its duty and to show Sandra's husband what fucking is.

Half stands by compliantly, taking pictures of a stranger penetrating and jamming his cock deep into his wife.

"Yes!" she demands, "just like that!"

I spread her legs wide and push my groin towards her, making sure that I push into her pussy walls.

She moans with a deep growl while I grab her ankles, so I can deeply access her vagina. I pile drive her, thrusting myself fully inside her, intending to split her in half.

"Give me the champagne," I command to Half, this time me giving orders. It's poetic, now I'm not only cuckolding his wife, but I'm also telling Half what to do.

He sheepishly hands it over to me.

I pour it over Sandra's body and it drips onto the bed, soaking it just like with her pussy juices. I pour more of the bottle into my mouth.

"Open up," I command Sandra, pouring the champagne into hers, she using her tongue to break up the flow of bubbles hitting her throat.

With a continuous motion, I slip my cock outside her and quickly saddle her and insert myself into her mouth, like a cock-chaser with the champagne.

Sandra is surprised. But then she slurps in delight as I see the tip of my cock pushing her cheek outwards.

I push in, fucking her mouth with fury, Sandra barely able to breathe as I hear her gagging.

I withdraw, Sandra panting a breath of fresh air now that she can.

I flip her, her hair now flying, and lock eyes with Half.

"Watch this," I directly say, "watch your wife fuck me."

I enter Sandra from behind so that Half has a full, unobstructed view of his wife in front of him.

I put my hands on the point where the waist meets the hips, that little curve. I start the motion, pulling her hips towards my cock, her ass jiggling as it hits my pelvis.

I withdraw my hands from her hips. "Your turn," I whisper in her ear, as I now use my free hands to sweep her hair up, her sweaty back getting a bit of respite.

Sandra complies, pushing herself into me, her ass shaking with ferocity, I pulling Sandra's hair like a tiny horse rein.

Slap, slap, slap, she pushes backwards, the slapping sound the only sound we hear in the room. She quickens the slaps. Harder.

Slap. Slap. Slap.

Her pussy swallows my entire cock, it sliding smoothly inside, like a piston pumping.

Slap. Slap. Slap.

I stroke my fingertips along her back.

"Uuuuhhhhhhhh uggghhhh," she pants.

Slap. Slap. Slap.

"Yeesssssss yeessss," she now moans, her voice punctuated by the slaps her ass makes by driving into my cock. Her fingers grasp the bed sheets in front of her.

Slap. Slap. Slap.

Beads of sweat at the small of her back, I careful to protect her curvy, perfumed hair from it. She lies flat, my 8 inches the only

thing connecting us between our two bodies.

"I'm cummmmmminggggggg...."

7

A Spritz

Panda lets me know last minute.

"A new girl!" she types, as I'm taking the limo to the hotel from Shenzhen Baoan airport. "Are you free tonight?"

I had just come from Beijing. I had hardly any sleep the night before, with too much drinking with potential venture capital investors. They had serious money, which explains my excessive drinking. And my flight this morning was at 5:30 AM.

I head over to the 7-11 for some easy liquor. Panda told me something casual would be appropriate.

She always makes vague, but accurate, references.

I grab a few cheap aluminium canned spritzers that contrast against my expensive steeled Rolex GMT. Easy drinking, easy from last night.

I enter the room. Alena is there, a relatively plain face, slightly plump body, the curves in the right places, deceptively pretty. She's not the classic pretty, but she's got the right angles everywhere.

But it is what she is wearing that is turning me on.

She puts her glasses up. Her hair in a bun. A white top, buttoned up. A blue mini skirt.

She has that schoolgirl look. An Asian schoolgirl.

My mind wanders - back to those teenage fantasies, the Japanese uniforms, the knee-high socks. I've never had this fantasy achieved before, and for it to be available now makes my mouth dry in anticipation.

Meanwhile, her innocent, black eyes stare back at me, waiting for me to do what I will.

* * *

I offer the canned spritzers to Alena. She pops one open, startled at the fizz creeping out of the opening.

She takes a drink. "I like it, it's kinda sweet," she chirps happily.

I'm glad. We take a few more swigs, using the drink as both foreplay and social lubricant.

"Take one more drink," I offer. I want her to get used to my

do," as I tease my cock in front of her face, prying her mouth open, gently forcing my way in.

I thrust more now, vigorously. I can see Alena is on the verge of gagging, but she mouths my cock and takes it all in.

She looks at me still, with the eyes of a pleasing girl, my hand gently caressing her head with care.

Gag. Gag. I hear her gagging, but she doesn't stop. Alena is in a daze now, fixated on my pleasure despite her physical protestations.

The more I gently stroke her hair, the more I violently thrust inside. Yin and Yang. Her eyes still look up at mine, those large moon eyes.

That's a good girl. Time to ratchet it up.

* * *

I withdraw from her sweet warm mouth, and with her schoolgirl clothes still on, I flip her skirt and take off her pink panties with a bow.

I love her choice of panties. It's cute, totally in line with her character as a schoolgirl. She could have just worn some Sailor Moon ones and that would make the role play complete, I think to myself.

I bring her panties up to my nose.

69

I take a whiff - her panties, sweet with her scent, sweet with innocence and nervousness. A bit of dampness, her pussy juices wetting the pink, making it a shade and shape of a red flower.

A flower to be deflowered by me.

Her pussy, freshly shaven and without a single hair, looks at me. It's so beautiful, the perfect labia size, the pink, the vagina slightly wet.

I really cannot help myself with a shaved pussy.

She looks into me with innocent eyes and nervous energy, wondering if she can take in my entire cock in her pussy.

I enter her with my size, immediately expanding her walls.

I fuck her for one thrust. Two. But my size is causing her discomfort.

"Take it," I say. Now I'm desperate to push her.

"No...," she says.

"You have to," I say. Like a good girl.

She wants to comply, not wanting to disappoint me.

And I will take her. I will claim her. I will claim her innocence.

"I know," I think to myself, "I know what to do."

I'm about to cum. I keep increasing the pace, my balls now slapping into her, I loving the feeling and sound of it as it hits her ass.

I release. My cum shoots into her.

Alena immediately opens her eyes, one part astounded by my audacity, another part enjoying the warmth coursing inside her, a third part the thought of sperm entering her body.

She pushes me, wanting to stop the flow of ejaculate. I over-power her, grasping her hips even harder, ensuring that she takes all my cum, every single drop.

"Take it," I command, "take it all."

"No, I can't", she gasps, "nooooo."

She accepts it now, her grip now loosening, unable to sway my conviction and my cock.

My cock unleashes wave after wave into her, mixing with her pussy juices and innocence, she powerless to stop, willing to receive me and my energy.

8

The G&T

It's been a long week.

We had a meeting this early afternoon at a very deep-pocketed Emirati family office. It was an absolutely critical meeting and we had to nail it.

Dubai would not be my normal stop, but my existing investor made a warm intro and the company will need the money soon in about a year. So it's never too soon to build and work on the relationship.

After the meeting, I have to breakaway from my team. Bless them they're great, but I need some alone time. Something to take my mind away.

I order a G&T at the Nobu bar in Dubai on Friday. It's too hot here, I already having abandoned my Richard Anderson suit jacket. I need something to cool down with, both physically and mentally. It's 8 PM, things already in full swing.

Great DJ. Great vibe. Great drink.

There's something great about a G&T. You can dress it up with better, more expensive gins or tonic waters, more exotic and more fragrant, or just go simple and cheap as chips. And tonight it's just cheap as chips so I can down as many as I can.

My issues with the client disappear as I look out towards the waters, Dubai towers lighting up the sky, the Armani hotel behind me.

I see a girl dancing next to the DJ. Brunette. A bob. Nice white blouse, black skirt. Tori Burches.

I get the vibes of a management consultant. BCG type. Intellectual.

She reminds me of someone. An old flame? An old colleague?

I'm searching my mind's Rolodex to see where it could be. Perhaps back at Uni? Or the disco.

She sees me staring at her.

She catches my eye. She saunters over, either because of me or that she's looking for a drink. I'd like to think it's the former.

I smell her perfume. J'adore. I love it.

"Hi there," I offer, not too eager. A thrust of a response.

"Hi back," she ripostes, "I'm Jasmine."

English. A bit posh.

I take all the cues in. Probably Oxbridge. Probably has a steady boyfriend, but hasn't seen much of him recently with her work. Overworked, undersexed. Definitely BCG, Senior analyst, or Associate. Not Partner.

"Come here much?" I ask.

"Not likely as often as you," she responds, smile cracking slightly.

I like a bit of banter. Spices up the conversation.

Our chat continues. How long are you going to be in Dubai? Who's your client? Enjoying it?

I touch her hand. Just briefly. A glancing connection. Just trying to connect.

She takes my hand.

* * *

Jasmine's taking me somewhere.

We go to the toilet, where there's no female or male side, but a shared communal sink. One of those very modern types of bathrooms.

She pulls my trousers down, my soldier springing forth. In her Tori Burches, she squats down.

She swallows my cock whole. Eagerly, passionately, hungrily.

It's been a while since one of these sessions, probably around my Uni days. But it's always nice to play like this.

The sound of the DJ, the beat of the music, the sensations of my cock being pleasured by a girl I just met a few moments ago.

Jasmine eagerly moves along my shaft, her mouth swallowing my whole organ over and over. Her mouth, smooth and warm, focused on my pleasure, as my dick seems to get harder and harder.

It's time.

I bring Jasmine up, turning her over, and flip up her black skirt. I take her panties, black as well, down to her ankles.

I put my fingers inside my mouth, lubricating them slightly before putting them inside her cooch.

God she's wet already.

I lean Jasmine on the bathroom door, inserting my bareback penis inside her, doggy style.

Her face is flat against the bathroom door, her hands pushing off it, her ass sticking out to receive me.

I thrust inside, pounding from behind, her ass cheeks absorbing my each and every push, my force jiggling her ass every single time I thrust.

There's something about raw, primal sex, without abandon, but muted with our voices as we channel energy just for sex. Just for fucking.

And seeing her face want to express the satisfaction of a cock filling her, but stopping shy of that. Her eyes closed, her mouth opened, but no sound coming out, just the absolute ecstasy and enjoyment of me thrusting inside her.

Suddenly, Jasmine stops. We hear two voices.

* * *

"Where is Jasmine..." they say, in their received pronunciation. One voice is posh, the other even more posh.

I'll name them Posh and Posher.

Jasmine is still. She does not move. At all.

Ah, so her name is Jasmine after all.

"Did she just leave with that bloke," Posh says.

"He was cute, wasn't he," Posher responds.

Ah, I get it. It's her friends.

"This could be fun," I think to myself.

I'm in her, her ass in front of me, her full and lovely ass. And I start my pumping again, this time with rhythm.

Jasmine looks back at me with a mix of horror and horniness.

"She can be such a slut sometimes," Posh offering, possibly applying some lipstick.

I pump, ensuring my full cock and base is entirely inside her. Slowly, slowly, inside.

"Yeah," Posher retorts, "I wonder what her body count is."

I pump more, increasing my speed slightly. Jasmine looks back again, biting her lip.

"Oh for sure more than 10," Posh replies, "wasn't there a guy just two weeks ago at the W?"

"Naughty girl," I whisper inside Jasmine's ear, "was he a good fuck like me?"

Jasmine doesn't respond. She doesn't need to.

I pump furiously now, increasing my cock reach inside her, holding her throat as another anchor to pull myself into her.

For the slut she is.

Jasmine's brunette hair bobs up and down, her ass jiggling from the pounding.

Posher replies, "Yeah, it was just a short fling, but they definitely were fucking!"

I increase my aggression, knowing that another man had violated her just recently. I determinedly want her to remember me, making this a moment she can't forget.

I thrust more aggressively, like an animal in heat. Thrust so far deep inside she can feel me, to pound her for the dirty girl she is. For my sperm to ejaculate deeper into her than the other guy.

It's not far enough. I want deeper.

I bend her down, Jasmine's hands on the floor, she pushing off it for support. Her pussy lips are now obvious and apparent, looking directly at me, beautiful and full.

"Yes," I think, "this is really deep now."

I slam myself in, each thrust timing to the DJ's techno beat, each downbeat, each boom. Then boom. Then boom.

I see Jasmine's face wretch with the unbridled pleasure that cannot be spoken or shouted out. She has to take it. Take each and every thrust inside her, to contain all the energy she wants to release, inside her body.

I quicken my pace, close to cumming, but wanting to give her a

few more thrusts inside.

Boom boom boom, with the DJ beat. Boom boom boom.

I withdraw quickly, just in time in fact. I cum on her ass, my white jizz decorating it like cream on an ass cake, as my waves of ecstasy matches with the music in the background.

9

A Yuzu Spritz

Taipei. I love this season. Rainy. The pitter-patter. The dampness.

But I don't like typhoons.

I was supposed to leave later tonight after my meetings, but because of the typhoon, my flight is delayed for another 24 hours. I should know what time I'm going to fly tomorrow.

That's the thing about typhoons. You just can't count what will happen with them. The eye could fly straight through the city and everything would be fucked. Or the eye could narrowly miss and all is averted.

So the only thing to do is to wait and see.

That's the thing with Mother Nature sometimes. As much as we believe it's our fate and we control it, Mother Nature turns right back and tells us she's in charge. And you better wait.

But everything seems ok now. A little rain. A little wet. That's about it.

What a bummer to cancel my flight on a Friday. I had everything planned for the weekend.

Now I don't even know when I'll head home.

I check the Hotel Proverbs concierge on what is open for dinner. Not all restaurants are open, afterall it is in the middle of a typhoon. I figured I shouldn't be too picky on what I'm having.

The concierge suggests a close-by izakaya place, for skewers. That's a good suggestion. Japanese cuisine is quite decent in Taiwan. They've retained some of the elements of their former colonists.

I check Google Maps. It's literally 3 minutes away, a left and a right.

Screw the umbrella.

I fold the sleeves of my previously creased crisp white collared dress shirt to highlight my Pepsi GMT. I head over to my early meal, brushing off the raindrops on my head.

It's a modern restaurant. Fancy, sleek interior, with deep bass beats pumping throughout the venue.

There's a bit of a bustling crowd, the venue is full. I suppose it's everyone that wants a meal and can't find open restaurants.

Full, except for a few seats. All at the bar.

The front of house mentions my name. It turns out the hotel had already reserved something for me.

Very thoughtful of them.

As we walk along the bar, I see a few reserved tags on the plates of a few empty seats.

She sits me down next to a young lady.

A. L. I. C.E. On her Casetify case.

* * *

Alice. I like that name.

Skinny. Real skinny. Long hair. Petite. Clothes, nothing to write home about, glasses.

Not my usual type.

But her tattoos. Loads of them. There's one on her upper arm. One on the back of her neck. One slightly covered by her crop top, but there.

And who knows what's on the lower half of her body.

She seems like a creative girl. Arts. Counter culture. Something like that.

Alice sucks from the top of the straw of her highball glass, the reddish, orange liquid accelerating right up to her lips.

The liquid goes into her mouth, a lump forming in her throat, and the same lump disappearing down her sleek neck as she sucks more and more.

Alice catches the eye of the bartender, tapping the now empty glass on the top of the rim.

Her fizzy drink, adorned in a tall highball glass with a pinkish, translucent color arrives. The bartender offers a smile as it is served.

Ni hao, I offer. Hello in Mandarin.

She looks at me, giving me no information whether she understood me or not.

I switch to English.

"I hope you don't mind me asking, but what are you drinking?" I ask, "It looks delicious."

"Yuzu spritz," she replies back, "yuzu is a tropical fruit, native for this region."

Her English is passable. Slight American accent.

"May I," and before she gets to reply, I have my straw at the ready to dab the drink for a taste.

"Sure," she replies. But I'm already dipping the shaft into the drink.

I press the top of the straw, creating the suction required to retain a bit of the spritz.

I withdraw and place a few drips on the back of my hand. I lick it.

Cold. Refreshing. Bubbly.

Yum. It's great.

"Bartender - may I have one as well?"

* * *

Alice is skinny. Real skinny. Petite. A-cup breasts.

Not all men like skinny girls. Most prefer full breasts. Or hips.

But skinny girls have their perks. They may not have full breasts, but their perky A-cups are just as sensitive.

You can't handle them by the handful, but you surely can pleasure them with your fingers.

Sure they have less cushion. But every thrust counts, every thrust hits deep.

Every push can be made to feel more impactful. Harder. Deeper.

Skinny girls are also a lot more flexible. You can pummel them in so many more ways. You can hold her ankles only, or spread her legs apart, or fold her legs up over her head and pile drive her.

I lightly touch Alice's cooch as I kiss her as I haven't kissed in a while, both of us standing.

She has a slight cigarette breath from the fag she just inhaled.

And she's shaved. For me.

A wetness seeps out of her vagina, slightly sticky.

But the cooch is lonely. It needs my fullness. That's really what I want.

I insert my two fingers in, my index and ring fingers. I push them through, all the way up her sticky, slippery hole.

The only fleshy part of her otherwise skinny pelvis and ass.

They stay in. Motionless. Just inside.

She gasps, opening her mouth. "Mmmm," she says, "oooohhh..."

Yes, I think to myself. Perfect.

I stay inside for good measure, enjoying the warmth and wetness and for her to enjoy my fullness. To get used to my

size and me inside her.

I withdraw and push her onto the white, creaseless bed.

In one motion I spread her skinny legs, folding her up by the stomach, compacting her like a pretzel.

I pile drive her.

She's so wet that she doesn't need me to direct my cock in. It just slides in, like a jackhammer intensely pounding the pavement.

I pound vertically into her again and again, my ass high up in the air, pile-driving directly into her, deep into her cervix.

It's a fucking great workout for me. And fullness for her. Extreme fullness.

"Ahh," she cries, "*hun dah!*" So big!

I continue my thrusts, my thighs working in overdrive, my hips folding and pushing and pounding.

But I want more.

I whip my cock out of her pussy, my tool springing out with a "pop".

I toss Alice in front of me.

I position myself behind her, putting myself deep into her, the

base of my cock hitting her bony ass.

Alice looks back at me, her hair whipping to one side, her eyes connecting with mine.

"*Gan wo. Gan wo!!!*" Fuck me, she speaks to me, Chinese dirty talk with those whorish, dazed eyes.

Yes, madam.

I withdraw and flip her over again, on a fresh corner of the bed that's not already wet with her sweat and pussy juice.

I spread her legs apart again, putting myself in and splitting her deep inside, my thighs and hips repeating the same motion that hit Alice's cervix so deep she cries out.

"Oooh," she screams, "*wo lai leh....*" I'm cumming, she moans out.

Her throaty voice adding energy to my thrusting, as if an equestrian is beating my ass for my full fucking effort.
    I continue to pile drive, my thighs getting a workout, my full weight through my cock plunging into her.

"*Ma leh,*" she says, oh my God....

We fuck for 2 hours like this. I splitting her in front with her legs as wide as possible, moving around on the bed, and then behind her deep with hard thick thrusts, on the side, her hanging on to the room chair.

I must have split Alice in half, her back in sweat, her eyes glossed over, in a daze at being fucked continuously over and over.

A pattern of being fucked, being used, being a subject of my aggression, my manhood, my pleasure.

10

A Singha

I'm in Bangkok for a bit of R&R after a long road show. And the city is always great with loads of massages available, everything from foot to head to 4 hands body. It's also the rainy season, which runs roughly from the end of May to September.

Bangkok can be dreadfully draining. Every night can be a night to enjoy, to party, to celebrate. The Thais certainly do.

So best to avoid the beers and the festivities. I'd rather not party with the backpackers and those here for the weed anyways. And one can only go to Soho House so many times.

Thankfully, this weekend, my friend booked me an overnight train to Chiang Mai.

Some of my other friends had warned me not to go for the train. That it's old and decrepit. Imagine the Indian trains, they say, from that era.

But it's a nostalgic habit from growing up in the UK. We used to take the train from London to the Cotswolds.

The rhythm of the carriage, the back and forth of the body as it moves with the train. The enjoyment of the scenery, stimulating the visual senses. A wine whilst looking outside, elevating the senses while dampening the monkey mind of daily worries and stresses.

It's a feast for all the senses.

I dress up for the occasion, with my Rolex GMT, white dress shirt and khaki slacks, navy blue Richard James sports jacket, and Oliver Peoples sunglasses. Like a proper gentleman.

I had splurged on the luxury car with my private room. Which really doesn't cost that much, around $50.

I leave my apartment with a weekender bag, hop on the Grab bike ride to the Krung Thep Aphiwat Central Terminal Station, ready for the adventures to come.

* * *

I quickly jump on the carriage and settle into my air-conditioned room.

Luckily I'm travelling at night, otherwise the stifling Bangkok heat would already get me hot and sticky. And it makes you wonder how life was without air conditioning.

I hang up my Tom Ford jacket and roll up the sleeves to my dress shirt, highlighting the tanned arms from my time in Bangkok whilst the GMT hangs loosely at the end of my wrist.

I head over to the diner car. A few cars away.

The plan is to hit dinner early, grab a pad thai or pad siew, a few beers, and read my novel as I drown my thoughts away. Get into my zone so no pesky backpacking *farang*, or foreigner, bother me asking about the latest weed or woke ideas.

But as they say, all plans are subject to change.

The car's nearly empty, me having come early. Likely the other *farang* are still unpacking or doing their travel vlog content. Good.

Nearly empty. Except for one girl.

A pretty one. Thai. Alone. By herself.

Slightly demure, with a black and white sweater over a casual khaki green dress. Underneath the sweater, her perky C-cup breasts peak out of the dress, the side cleavage revealing smooth, white skin.

I can tell she's got great assets, but she wants to keep them hidden away.

The green dress runs down to half her thighs, exposing her long smooth legs, cross legged and ending with her sparkling

toenails.

Her hair, flawless. Her face, cute, with high cheekbones, strong nose, and thick lips. The lips I love.

She's looking at her phone. Lost in her social media. Tik Tok or something or other.

She looks up at me. Looks back down at her phone.

They say Thais are addicted to social media. She probably is as well then.

I look at her briefly, deliberating whether to stick to my plan of silent solitude and intellectual exploration or be preposterously polite and great company.

Fuck it. I choose the latter.

Sawadi-krap. Hello.

I ask her whether she's alone. She looks up. Nods. And goes back to her phone.

I'm slightly perturbed by her dismissiveness. But you never know, and hey, there could be a language barrier.

I sit down, my khaki slacks folding underneath on the ancient diner carriage seats, the GMT bracelet lightly tapping the top of the table.

"What's your name," I ask gently.

"JB," she replies, a cute, high-toned voice, a very pleasant tickling on the ears.

I don't ask further on actually what JB stands for, not wanting to offend.

We talk a bit, her English not as confident. But I'm sure enough is there.

"Where are you from," I ask, half-knowing the answer through an educated guess. She's probably heading home, travelling by herself.

"Chiang Mai," she offers back.

"Great. I'm getting a beer, a Changi. Would you like one?" I ask as I prepare to stand up and head to the bar.

She laughs, covering her smile with her petite hand, either to hide my shame or hers.

"Changis are for *farang.* Drink Singha."

Right.

* * *

We're 4 beers in. Each. JB's been pouring the beers furiously, making sure my cup is always full.

If I were a betting man, I would bet she's trying to make me drunk.

We discuss Thai food and culture, the route to Chiang Mai, and the things to do there. Typical foreigner discussion, but I try to make things entertaining, sometimes feigning ignorance.

Do Thai girls like foreign men? Do they sleep with them on the first date?

She loves to say no to me. JB slaps me on my non-GMT hand across the table when I say something silly.

She looks at me directly with her flirty eyes, her brown irises communicating her energy and liveliness directly to mine.

It's not the words that are spoken that explain the connection.

Underneath the table is where the action is.

JB continuously touches my leg with hers under the table. Her leg moves upwards to my crotch, playing around at my groin area. It glances at my lengthening girth, I can feel her individual toes as if they're stroking my cock.

I don't reveal much and remain stoic. A man needs to be sure when bedding a woman. So let her keep feeding signals until it's inevitable.

But until then - don't start too soon.

Make her want it.

I bring the 5th bottle of Singha up to my lips, to the bottom of my pursed lips, about to take a swig to lengthen the quiet between us.

Sometimes, no words need to be said. And to just savour the moment.

"What is your size?" she whips out, "and circumference?"

I make horizontal the Singha to swallow my slight surprise, giving me time to recover and come up with a worthy response.

"What do you do again?" I smile slightly.

"Only Fans," she whips back.

"Right," I retort, "have you ever made content on a train?"

* * *

We make it back to my private train room without anyone noticing JB furiously stroking my cock underneath my khaki slacks.

During our conversation she had told me Thai guys are too gentle. Too nice. Too polite.

They don't fuck her the way she likes to be fucked.

As a gentleman, of course I aim to please. And I too can be an aggressive fuck.

She unbuttons the top of my waistband, forcing the zipper down to its limit, then pulling down both slacks and underwear in one go.

Greedy girl.

Out pops my erect cock, pink and warm as it stands ready for action, nearly poking her in the eye. She giggles.

JB caresses my cock with her warm, smooth petite hand, and guides it into her warm, luscious mouth. She sucks at it eagerly, slurping and popping with delight.

"Oh yesssss," I share, letting her know much I'm enjoying it. And I'm not kidding, she's good.

JB continues, sucking with conviction, as if she hasn't eaten cock in weeks. She does it with an eagerness and a desire, deep-throating me to my base.

Now's my turn. Let's turn it up a notch.

I pick JB up by cute little ass and toss her onto the carriage bed. Her small frame is easy to play around with. Just my type.

I hitch up the dress, tearing off her panties, revealing her beautiful, bare snatch. Super smooth.

I don't care about the green or the sweater, I really don't.

I force her legs as wide as I can, opening her pussy wide to my desires. I want that pussy to feast on.

I tongue her hot, bare snatch. No hair whatsoever, super smooth. I love that.

"Oooh," she coos.

I can tell JB likes my aggression, her not resisting but leaning into my every move, every action.

And I do as well. I love someone who loves sex as much as I do.

I keep tongue fucking her, eager to get it all inside. It's so tasty, her pussy. Oh it's so good.

Her thin labia lips, her small little hole, just starting to secrete a little of her sex.

I eagerly suck her juice, suck her clit, and suck whatever I can of her little pussy hole.

But now I want to see her breasts. Those C cups that flirted with me before.

I pop open the sweater and cinch her green dress past her naked ass, off her legs.

Those C cups, perky and full, waiting to be tasted.

I can't resist. I plunge into her chest, sucking those round, little tits.

I suck JB's brown little ones perched on top of her full, round C-cup mounds. I grab her breasts by the handful, releasing her long, thin legs.

But it's time now to have my dick feel her pussy.

I push her thin smooth legs up, up over her head, pushing and squishing her tits closely. Her small hole is now fully exposed to me, waiting to receive me and my cock.

"Fuck me," JB moans as she looks wantonly into my eyes, "fuck me..."

I don't need her to roll out the red carpet for me.

I violently plunge myself into her pussy, her pussy walls smooth with her wetness. Just the once. And I stay there.

To get her deep, as deep as she can handle. And more. To give her my fucking.

Because she wants it. Because she's a naughty girl. She's a slut.

I begin my rhythmic thrusts. Once. Every. Second.

She loves that.

"Yessss," JB moans, "fuuucckkk!"

I plunge my thick, hot cock into her wet, slick pussy, time after time. Quicker now.

My balls slap into her ass as I do. Bam bam bam.

The sound that any man, any person will recognize. The sound of love.

"Fuck," JB screams, "fucckkk!!!"

She's clearly enjoying it. She loves my cock, my aggression, the feeling of me deep inside her.

But I want more. I want deeper. I want her to remember me.

I flip her over. I spit into her ass hole, licking it for good measure too.

"Ooooohhh," she moans surprisingly, not expecting that I would have the audacity to play with her ass.

I push my thick cock directly into her asshole. It pushes deep, filling her ass, widening her hole. But I know she's enjoying it. Enjoying my thickness, my largeness.

I thrust again inside her, enjoying the tightness, penetrating deeper into her.

"Deeper," she cries, "in meeee!"

Pump, pump, pump. My hips don't stop.

"Yessss!", she looks back me, her eyes meeting mine, "like that!!"

I want to cum. To enjoy this. To have my own pleasure.

I withdraw. I grab her head by her hair, cupping the base of her skull.

"Suck me off," I command her, "suck me dry."

JB complies, quickly kneeling towards my head, her mouth wide open as her slutty eyes pierce directly into mine.

Just as my dick starts to convulse, JB's beautiful lips clamp down on my cock like a vice, taking it all in as she purses her lips and sucks.

Her beautiful lips suck me dry of all my semen, sucking all the juices up, like the good slut she is.

11

A Nightcap

I'm in Barcelona a few days early. I'm to speak at a major tech conference later in the week, but I figured I would stop by early to enjoy the city.

I love Barcelona - it's a city with amazing energy. You can just feel it, touch it, smell it.

I'm staying at a boutique hotel this time, the Sir Victor, as a welcome change to the usual Ibis or other business hotels.

I saunter towards check-in, my Rolex GMT oyster bracelet pinging against the marbled desk. "*Passaporte, por favor,*" asks the attendant on the other side. Credentials please.

On my left strolls in a dirty blonde, about to do the same.

I carefully eye her up and down. A tall, slender girl, a brunette with streaks of blonde, very leggy, full ass, and toned body. She's wearing a tight-fitting work suit, which highlights the

fact that she works out.

Our eyes lock, her beautiful hazel irises looking into mine.

I withdraw, slowly, to linger, but not to be too hasty.

"Russian. German?" I think to myself. I hope to see more of her.

I head upstairs to my sparse, but modern room.

I take a shower to settle down. I can't sleep, perhaps a bit too wired from the travel, perhaps I'm channelling the energy of the city. I've already eaten on the plane so no more tapas and cava for me now.

"Maybe I go swim in the pool," I think, trying to find ways to come off my traveling high.

I change into my Vilebrequins, the quick drying, travel-friendly brand.

I wear my slippers. I go upstairs. Into the fresh air.

* * *

It's quiet up here. 10 PM according to my Breitling. I didn't manage to bring my Rolex, nor do I want to bring it as it's a bit too flashy for European travel.

Quiet. Except for the dirty blonde doing laps.

She's now adorned with a sharp dark one-piece swimsuit. Her body is sleek, slim, toned, her strokes immaculate, her wake sleek and gentle. She glides over the water, her fingertips caressing the water as they enter, cupping it gently.

By the looks of it, she's a serious swimmer.

Well, I'm serious too.

I dive into the pool. It's been a while since my triathlon training, but I vaguely recall how to swim fast. The key is gliding, to spread yourself into the water, immersing into and becoming one.

I catch up to the dirty blonde, she to my left. I stretch myself, gasping for air, and front crawl. I inch ahead of her.

"Here comes the turn," I remind myself as I look slightly ahead, thinking to tuck in, roll, and push off the block. As I said, it's been a while.

I lose whatever advantage I had. I clumsily accelerate off the block, she already executing it, clearly knowing what to do.

She's back on top. As if she knows I'm trying to beat her.

I go all out, pumping my back muscles and lungs, reminding myself to glide, but wanting to pump my strokes.

My lungs burn. My legs kick. My thighs tight.

I stretch towards the last 10 metres. Glide. Out. Now!

I see the blonde touching the wall just after me.

She surfaces for air, her mouth open, gasping, passionate. She lost, and she yearns to know who has beaten her.

* * *

"Good swim," I say to the dirty blonde smugly, hinting my dominance.

She asks me my name. I tell her a fake one.

"I'm Leena," she offers.

"Perhaps it's a fake one too," I think.

Leena's high from competition, her tits still moving up and down as she sucks in air. I imagine the beautiful breasts underneath that suit, dark nipples that I can suck.

I see her tattoos, one on the inside of her arms, the other underneath the water near her hips. I can't quite make out what they say, but I'm intrigued.

"Definitely Russian," I think.

She's here for a conference, a tech one. I think I know the one. I saw the posters as I was arriving.

"How did you get so competitive?" I ask, eager to know where she got her fire from.

She's an ex volleyball player. Played competitively for her country.

"That explains her body," I say to myself, taking in her beautiful form, her lovely face, her long, sinewy arms. She's still super fit, proud of her own body, someone who's in touch with it and knows what it needs and desires.

But it's her energy that draws me closer. It's something about her, maybe something about the competition, something raw.

I wade a little closer, my confidence high from winning the small competition, eager to get to know her.

We both had let our guards down, into the water, feeling the passion of the moment as we swam side by side. We were connected, through spirit, through the water, through competition.

And now that energy draws me close. Draws me closer to her body.

Our bodies meet. They touch.

I grab her hips. I kiss her passionately.

* * *

Leena accepts me. She slips her tongue inside my mouth as I enter hers, my hand cradling the back of her head.

We embrace, our energies colliding, as if we've always known each other but having never met.

My hand searches for her ass, her back, something to pull her closer to me. I want her heart to feel mine, for our chests to join.

I kiss her, the kiss of a desperate man, searching for intimacy.

She emerges from our full kiss, gasping for air.

"I want your cock," she says out loud, "I want it now."

I scootch my ass up to the edge of the pool, on the stone. I comply, fumbling off my Vilebrequins, my cock bursting out.

Leena offers her pretty face to my soldier, taking it in, slurping and using her tongue to pleasure me.

I haven't been sucked off like this for a while. And not in public.

She continues with pace, puffing out her checks, looking into my eyes as she consumes with competitive ferocity.

It's as if I'm fucking a tight pussy, but the pussy is fucking me. Leena's lips touch the tip of my cock, smacking her lips when she tickles it.

I look up into the sky. The stars. The cool air. My cock being

107

pleasured. The feeling is surreal.

"I'm going to cum," I tell her, "Swallow me."

Leena looks compliantly into my eyes, accepting the mission.

I cum. It hits her everywhere, in her mouth, in the back of her throat, my warmth surging in her mouth. It fills her mouth, like warm cotton candy.

I lean closer to Leena, looking deeply into her eyes as she swallows. This dirty blonde goddess, my dirty blonde goddess.

She does it so confidently and authoritatively, clearly a pro.

I withdraw from her mouth, my limp dick falling under its own weight on the stone with a thump, dry from being sucked clean.

I caress Leena's head carefully. I kiss her.

I taste my own cum as I taste her mouth. It's delicious, a potent mix of sex, saliva, and semen.

12

A Nightcap Part 2

It's Leena's final day in Barcelona.

I had taped us fucking and she didn't know it. And now I send her those videos via Whatsapp, a side view of me fucking her from behind and on top, her moaning and cursing like a slut.

"Make sure you put your headphones on," I tease.

She immediately types back.

"You fucking bastard. You're making me wet 🐇"

* * *

Leena texts.

"I'll be there in 1 hour. Go shower now"

Ok, I think. What's going on here.

About 15 minutes later, "go downstairs and ask the concierge for some candles ❤."

15 minutes now.

I reply cheekily, "Is there some more?"

She replies.

"Go back to your room and light the candle ♨."

I comply, heading back to Mr. Porter.

15 minutes left.

"Undress down to your boxers and turn your door lock so the door doesn't close. Turn off the lights and put on some *Cigarettes After Sex* ▥".

I do, gently setting the Pepsi GMT aside.

She opens the door of the room.

* * *

She comes into the room. Takes off her bathrobe. And reveals her lace, black lingerie with suspenders.

She passes by the wardrobe, where my suits and dress shirts are hung. She grabs my two ties, both Drakes, my favourites. I don't bring them often, but I'm glad I did today.

She comes over to the bed and pushes me over. I land, softly on the pillows, feigning submission.

She comes over, like a devil of sex, straddling me. I can feel the warmth of her mound on my belly. I can smell her sex. I love it.

She ties my left hand first with my green tie to the bedpost with a makeshift knot, and my right hand with my favourite, my all red.

I feign like I can't get myself out. But honestly, she's tied it pretty securely.

"Ouch," I say, "it's a bit tight."

"Of course it is," she orders right back.

I like the authority.

Her tying done, she moves down to my hip area, removing my silk boxers. My cock springs out from them, standing erect, at attention.

She moves back up, looking at me with those beautiful and sexy eyes. She kisses me now, thrusting her tongue inside my mouth. It's warm, sweet, with a slight candy taste.

She withdraws, licking me from neck down, slowly moving to my nipples and sucking them with care.

She licks the centre of my chest, then down, down, towards the

direction of my dick.

She ends with confidence, popping my full cock right inside her mouth.

"Oh......" I moan.

She comes right up.

"Not so fast," she commands at me. "Just you wait, big boy."

Leena grabs the lit candle now that's beside the bed post. The wax is plentiful, moving and shaking as she moves the candle from post to above me.

"Relax, big boy. It'll hurt just a little bit," she teases.

She tips the candle slightly, the watery wax dripping onto my stomach.

It's surprising, a combination of the expectation of pain but yet not as much as I thought. Strongly comfortable.

"It's not so bad, you see," she delights, seeing me relax, "you'll grow to like it."

She pours some more. And some more.

The candle wax is everywhere on my torso, some on the lower part, some higher.

It feels nice, but the flame of the candle gets me anticipating pain every single time. My senses are tingled. Heightened.

She now moves to my cock. Finally.

With one hand she grabs my cock, the other hand she turns on her camera to video herself.

She just goes to town with my dick, slurping and sucking my servant of sex, whilst looking into the camera. The sounds of her honouring my tool are elevated, ensuring that the camera effectively captures her whole experience.

It's so hot.

She now releases her hand to play with my balls, her other hand still capturing the video.

She loves to eat cock, this one.

She puts down the camera on one side of my leg.

She then sits up, straddling my crotch. She puts me into her, reverse cowgirl.

I feel huge. Inside her pussy walls. Inside her hot, throbbing body, filling her inside.

The selfie camera goes on again, videoing herself.

She grinds, moving back and forth, pleasuring herself as my

cock fills her. I can feel my cock just filling her, and she enjoying that fullness.

I love it, how she's so focused on her pleasure, disregarding me. I'm just a tool, a machine, for her pleasure that she's capturing for herself.

She pops up, my cock bursting out of her pussy, and turns around to face me.

"You want to see me now, don't you," she teases me.

I didn't mind either way. I just loved seeing her get off that I didn't care what view I had. But of course, seeing her tits doesn't hurt.

Leena lowers herself and pops herself back into my cock.

She rides me. Up and down, up and down. No lateral movement, just straight 8 inches into her, and 8 inches out.

I love that she's enjoying every inch of my length. As if she wants no other stimulation, just my cock, and feeling every inch of it inside her tight pussy walls.

Slap. Slap. Slap. The sound of her ass slamming into me every single time she enjoys those 8 inches of pleasure.

I see her face. Her beautiful tits. She's facing the camera, desperate for it to capture every second, every moment, every moan of this moment.

Slap. Slap. Slap. I love how she's squatting down hard, and how my cock just disappears right inside her.

Slap. Slap. Slap. Her eyes close, her dirty blonde hair flying up and down vertically, her toes curled up beside me.

"I'm cumming...."

* * *

She sends me the video of our sex. She's just left, straight to the airport to head back home.

"No man's ever cum inside of me. You're my first. This is my little present for you "

13

A Nightcap Part 3

After last night, I went straight to bed. It was very calm.

Do you know what it is like, as if I found someone whose soul and thoughts are connected with mine?

You think that this is some kind of fantasy. Well, I will say and I believe that this is fate.

I trust in fate and that it gives my will freedom.

* * *

In the morning I wake up and immediately go to the shower.

All the time HE is on my mind from last night. I want HIM so much. HIS huge beautiful cock, broad shoulders, and beautiful smile.

The thought that HE will fuck me this evening makes my hand go

down as the water trickles down the shower and to my mound.

I start playing with my pussy thinking about HIS hard cock. I rub my clit, thinking about how HE will spank my ass, how HE will take me doggy style and stick his dick in.

"No, that's not it. This is just a fantasy," I think to myself.

I turn off the water, take a towel and start drying myself, across my perky breasts, my hips, my legs. I take my favorite cream and spread it on myself with my right hand.

"I smell delicious," I think.

I spray myself with my favorite vanilla and coconut-scented spray and go out of the bath.

I put on my bright blue panties with lace, but not my bra, because I like it when my boobs are free.

* * *

I go to breakfast and get myself a salad with cucumbers and scrambled eggs. I don't like to eat too much in the morning.

The restaurant is very nice and cosy with huge windows.

I take my food and sit down next to one of the windows and start eating.

A minute later a young man comes up and asks if the seat next

to me is free. He is wearing a shirt and blue jeans.

At first glance, he is very handsome, blue eyes, blonde hair. My favorite type.

"I like him," I think.

He sits down.

He only takes a cup of coffee and a small cheesecake for himself. He starts eating and so do I. We look at each other and eat without saying a word.

It's a bit weird. Too weird for me because usually guys come and want to meet. This guy just sits in front of me and eats.

He eats his last piece, says thank you to me, and stands up.

Before he is about to leave the restaurant, I blurt out, "What is your name."

"Minho" he answers.

I go to the room to take my laptop to head to a meeting. I open the door and see a piece of paper on the floor.

A small yellow piece of paper. What could be written on it?!

"I saw everything." With love M.

And then I understand everything. Who he was, why he was

sitting next to me, and what he wanted from me.

* * *

In the evening after my meetings, I go for a drink. I go to the bar that was next to the hotel and get myself some white wine.

HE and Minho are sitting next to my table and locked in conversation about something. I enter and they don't notice me.

I am wet all day today after yesterday's sex in the pool. I start to think already slutty thoughts when I see them together.

I quickly slam four glasses of white wine and am already quite drunk. When I'm drunk my feelings are direct. Horny.

"That's it. I want both of them."

I walk up to them and sit in the middle without saying a word. With one hand I grab Minho's flaccid cock underneath his pants, with the other hand I take HIS hair and begin to suck his lips.

* * *

10 minutes later we find ourselves in HIS room.

I am drunk but it doesn't bother me at all and I start kissing them on the lips. Ahhhh, both are tasty.

They both undress me, Minho from the top, HE my bottom. They

furiously tear my clothes off, two tongues licking my tits and my whole body, from my neck down to my ankles.

Fuck, it feels great.

Ahhhhhh, and I'm so wet already

HE turns me around, bends me over, and puts his huge cock inside me. It hits me deep inside. His 8 inches filling me.

I want to cum!!!

At the same time I am sucking Minho's beautiful dick as I play with his balls, me getting banged from behind while I gag on his tool.

They are both great, but I like HIS cock more and decide to sit on it and ride it. I want to cum!!

I push my ass backward and sit down on HIS cock.

I start riding, HIS dick in and out of my wet, sloppy pussy. It's huge and hard. It thrusts inside me, like a machine, hitting my G spot.

In front Minho continues to lick my tits. He then sticks his cock inside my mouth again for good measure.

It feels so good.

I scream. They call me a whore and slut.

It makes me even hornier.

I hear the slapping as my ass hits HIS cock, and that makes me even hornier as I gag on Minho's giant cock in front of me.

This feels so good. Two cocks inside of me. Two big, fun cocks.

I'm such a slut.

We cum together.

HE cums inside me. I feel HIS hot, delicious sperm.

Minho withdraws from my mouth and cums on my tits.

I am covered in cum both inside and outside.

Fuck I love it, I want this to happen more often.💦💦

We go to the shower, bathe, and go to bed together.

I am in the middle. We are all naked. They hug me tightly and I feel the hot body of both.🔥

14

Double Trouble by Leena

After last night, I went straight to bed. It was very calm.

Do you know what it is like, as if I found someone whose soul and thoughts are connected with mine?

You think that this is some kind of fantasy. Well, I will say and I believe that this is fate.

I trust in fate and that it gives my will freedom.

* * *

In the morning I wake up and immediately go to the shower.

All the time HE is on my mind from last night. I want HIM so much. HIS huge beautiful cock, broad shoulders and beautiful smile.

The thought that HE will fuck me this evening makes my hand go

down as the water trickles down the shower and to my mound.

I start playing with my pussy thinking about HIS hard cock. I rub my clit, thinking about how HE will spank my ass, how HE will take me doggy style and stick his dick in.

"No, that's not it. This is just a fantasy," I think to myself.

I turn off the water, take a towel and start drying myself, across my perky breasts, my hips, my legs. I take my favorite cream and spread it on myself with my right hand.

"I smell delicious," I think.

I spray myself with my favorite vanilla and coconut scented spray and go out of the bath.

I put on my bright blue panties with lace, but not my bra, because I like it when my boobs are free.

* * *

I go to breakfast and get myself a salad with cucumbers and scrambled eggs. I don't like to eat too much in the morning.

The restaurant is very nice and cosy with huge windows.

I take my food and sit down next to one of the windows and start eating.

A minute later a young man comes up and asks if the seat next

to me is free. He is wearing a shirt and blue jeans.

At first glance he is very handsome, blue eyes, blonde hair. My favourite type.

"I like him" I think.

He sits down.

He only takes a cup of coffee and a small cheesecake for himself. He starts eating and so do I. We look at each other and eat without saying a word.

It's a bit weird. Too weird for me because usually guys come and want to meet. This guy just sits in front of me and eats.

He eats his last piece, says thank you to me, and stands up.

Before he is about to leave the restaurant, I blurt out, "what is your name."

"Minho" he answers.

I go to the room to take my laptop to head to a meeting. I open the door and see a piece of paper on the floor.

A small yellow piece of paper. What could be written on it?!

"I saw everything." With love M.

And then I understand everything. Who he was, why he was

sitting next to me and what he wanted from me.

* * *

In the evening after my meetings I go for a drink. I go to the bar that was next to the hotel and get myself some white wine.

HE and Minho are sitting next to my table and locked in conversation about something. I enter and they don't notice me.

After yesterday's sex in the pool I am wet all day today. I start to think already slutty thoughts when I see them together.

I quickly slam four glasses of white wine and am already quite drunk. When I'm drunk my feelings are direct. Horny.

"That's it. I want both of them."

I walk up to them and sit in the middle without saying a word. With one hand I grab Minho's flaccid cock underneath his pants, with the other hand I take HIS hair and begin to suck his lips.

* * *

10 minutes later we find ourselves in HIS room.

I am drunk but it doesn't bother me at all and I start kissing them on the lips. Ahhhh, both are tasty.

They both undress me, Minho from the top, HE my bottom. They

literally tear my clothes off, licking my tits and go down licking my whole body, from my neck down to my ankles.

Fuck, it feels great.

Ahhhhhh, and I'm so wet already✌

HE turns me around, bends me over, and puts his huge cock inside me. It hits me deep inside. His 8 inches filling me.

I want to cum!!!

At the same time I am sucking Minho's beautiful dick as I play with his balls, me getting banged from behind while I gag on his tool.

They are both great, but I like HIS cock more and decide to sit on it and ride it. I want to cum!!

I push my ass backwards and sit down on HIS cock.

I start riding, HIS dick in and out of my wet, sloppy pussy. It's huge and hard. It thrusts inside me, like a machine, hitting my G spot.

In front Minho continues to lick my tits. He then sticks his cock inside my mouth again for good measure.

It feels so good.

I scream. They call me a whore and slut.

It makes me even hornier.

I hear the slapping as my ass hits HIS cock, and that makes me even hornier as I gag on Minho's giant cock in front of me.

This feels so good. Two cocks inside of me. Two big, fun cocks.

I'm such a slut.

We cum together.

HE cums inside me. I feel HIS hot, delicious sperm.

Minho withdraws from my mouth and cums on my tits.

I am covered in cum both inside and outside.

Fuck I love it, I want this to happen more often.

We go to the shower, bathe and go to bed together.

I am in the middle. We are all naked. They hug me tightly and I feel the hot body of both.

15

Conclusion

I can tell you that the law of attraction is real.

The law of attraction is not just a philosophical theory or wishful thinking—there's a deep, underlying truth to the idea that the energy we project into the world shapes what we attract back into our lives. I've come to understand that this principle is most vividly seen in our connections with others, particularly in the realm of sexual attraction. Sexuality, being one of the most primal and core aspects of human nature, provides a raw and tangible way to experience how the Law of Attraction operates in its purest form.

At its core, the Law of Attraction works on the premise that like attracts like. We emit energy based on our thoughts, emotions, and beliefs, and that energy draws in experiences and people that resonate with it. You attract what you are, not just what you want. It's not enough to desire something if your internal state doesn't align with that desire. Instead, you have to cultivate the same frequency of energy that matches the things or people you

want to bring into your life.

In theory, this sounds simple: think positive, feel good, and you'll attract positive outcomes.

But in practice, it requires a deeper understanding of yourself, your needs, and the signals you're sending out into the world. The universe responds to the energy beneath your surface— what's really going on inside of you—not just the intentions you set or the affirmations you recite. It's about being in true alignment with what you seek.

The more I explored this idea, the more I began to see how it applies to relationships, especially sexual ones. Attraction is an energetic exchange, and sexual attraction, in particular, is a raw and instinctual form of this energy. The more sexual partners I met, the clearer this became. I wasn't just engaging in casual encounters; I was learning something fundamental about myself, my needs, and the people I was drawing into my life.

The fascinating part is that the more partners I met, the more I became in tune with what I needed from these connections. It wasn't just about physical attraction or chemistry—it was about understanding the energy that resonated with me and how I was aligning with others on a deeper level. Each experience revealed a little more about my true desires, and as I became more self-aware, I noticed that the people I attracted shared similar needs. This wasn't by chance; it was the Law of Attraction in action.

There's a subtle, almost instinctual way you start to grasp the

Law of Attraction through sexual experiences. You realise that sexual attraction isn't just a random, fleeting feeling—it's the most basic and primal manifestation of energy alignment.

It's a direct reflection of how your internal state attracts a corresponding external experience. If your energy is confident, self-assured, and open, you naturally attract partners who are on the same wavelength. Conversely, if you're uncertain, insecure, or disconnected from yourself, the people you meet often reflect that state, resulting in less satisfying or imbalanced interactions.

In a way, sexual attraction becomes the easiest and most direct way to learn about the Law of Attraction. Why? Because sexuality is such a natural, core part of who we are. It's an expression of our most basic desires and needs, stripped of pretence.

When two people connect on a sexual level, there's no room for inauthenticity—the energy exchange is raw and real.

You can feel when it's right, and you can feel when it's not. That instant recognition of alignment or misalignment is the Law of Attraction at work.

For many people, understanding the Law of Attraction can feel abstract or distant. But when it comes to sexual relationships, the principles are easier to see and feel. The attraction between two people is a living example of how energy draws energy. It's an undeniable, primal connection that's governed by the same laws that apply to every other aspect of life.

What I've come to understand is that sexual attraction serves as a mirror for the energy you're putting out into the world. It's one of the most transparent ways to see how your internal state manifests externally. Through these experiences, you start to see patterns—how your mindset and emotions influence the type of people you attract, and how your energy dictates the depth and quality of the connection.

In the end, the Law of Attraction is much more than a theoretical concept. It's a tangible force that you can feel and observe, especially in the realm of sexual attraction. The more I learned to tune into my own energy, the more I saw how my connections reflected my inner world.

Sexuality, being a primal part of human nature, offers one of the clearest, most immediate ways to understand this law. It's a fundamental part of who we are, and through it, we can begin to grasp how attraction truly works.

And here's the thing: you can experience this too. There is no better way to understand the Law of Attraction than to connect with your sexual energy, to really feel your desires and embrace them.

Sexuality is a natural, core part of who you are, and when you honour that, you start to tap into a powerful force. Don't be shy. Don't fear it. Embrace it.

Through sexual attraction, you'll start to see how the Law of Attraction works in its most primal, authentic form, and that understanding will ripple into every other area of your life.

About the Author

The Gentleman introduces *The Adventures of a Tech Casanova*, a tantalizing collection by an author who lives the life others only dream of. A tech billionaire with a taste for luxury and a talent for unforgettable encounters, he's no stranger to the world's finest hotels, most exclusive parties, and hidden pleasures. Each tale, inspired by his global travels and opulent lifestyle, unveils the seductive adventures that come naturally to a man of charm, wit, and endless ambition.

From the glittering heights of his high-tech empire to the intimate allure of Taipei, Tokyo, Barcelona, and Dubai, he brings readers into a world where every erotic experience is lived to the fullest—and every erotic story is meant to be shared.

www.ingramcontent.com/pod-product-compliance
Lightning Source LLC
Chambersburg PA
CBHW061523050726
47503CB00015B/2686